NOV - - 2019

Praise for

THE BISHOP'S BEDROOM

D0049949

"Chiara's engrossing novel of loafing lotharios in post-WWII Italy hums with suspense ... Readers will be swept away by this lush, gothic-tinged mystery and its unscrupulous characters."

—*PUBLISHERS WEEKLY*

"Chiara's brief masterwork turns insinuation into high art ... A first-rate book that is both a moody suspense novel and a haunting allegory."

—*KIRKUS REVIEWS* (Starred Review)

"I consider myself to be the son of Piero Chiara ... I was his devoted reader. I've always loved storytellers and Chiara had great powers of seduction."

—ANDREA CAMILLERI,
author of *The Shape of Water*

"For such a wicked and wanton novel, *The Bishop's Bedroom* is as tightly-controlled and queasily suspenseful as the best of Patricia Highsmith. It seduced me from its atmospheric opening pages to its shocking and satisfying final act."

—CHRISTOPHER CASTELLANI,
author of *Leading Men*

ESTES VALLEY
LIBRARY

"Piero Chiara's novel is at once a murder mystery and a lyrical study of desire, greed, and deception. The ending is simply stunning."

—ANDRÉ ACIMAN,
author of *Call Me by Your Name*

"Piero Chiara's dark idyll of erotic entanglements in post-WWII Italy was a revelation to me: a character study of sinister power, a beautiful evocation of the dolce vita on Lake Maggiore, and an unnerving portrayal of the predatory sexual mores of another world that mirrors those of our own in the strangest, most unexpected ways."

—JAMES LASDUN,
author of of *The Fall Guy* and *Give Me Everything You Have*

"An author universally known in Italy, who has received several literary prizes . . . esteemed as one of the most talented of modern novelists."

—*WORLD LITERATURE TODAY*

"One of Piero Chiara's masterpieces."

—*LA STAMPA*

"An erotic charge is ready to explode at any moment . . . One of the greatest works of 20th-century Italian literature."

—RENZO MONTAGNOLI

THE
BISHOP'S
BEDROOM

BY PIERO CHIARA

TRANSLATED FROM THE ITALIAN BY JILL FOULSTON

NEW VESSEL PRESS
NEW YORK

 New Vessel Press

www.newvesselpress.com

First published in Italian as *La stanza del Vescovo*

Copyright © 1976 Arnoldo Mondadori Editore S.p.A., Milano
Copyright © 2015 Mondadori Libri S.p.A., Milano

Translation Copyright © 2019 Jill Foulston

All rights reserved. Except for brief passages quoted in a newspaper, magazine, radio, television, or website review, no part of this book may be reproduced in any form or by any means, electronic or mechanical, including photocopying and recording, or by any information storage and retrieval system, without permission in writing from the Publisher.

Library of Congress Cataloging-in-Publication Data
Chiara, Piero
[La stanza del Vescovo. English]
The Bishop's Bedroom/ Piero Chiara; translation by Jill Foulston.
p. cm.
ISBN 978-1-939931-74-0
Library of Congress Control Number: 2019934492
I. Italy—Fiction

THE BISHOP'S BEDROOM

I

IN THE LATE AFTERNOON of a summer's day in 1946, I arrived at the port of Oggebbio on Lake Maggiore at the helm of a large sailboat. The *inverna* is a wind that rises from the Lombardy Plain every day during good weather and blows the entire length of the lake. Between noon and six o' clock it hadn't driven me any farther than that small lakeside village, so I decided to spend the night.

On board alone—as ever, it seemed—I struggled for half an hour to moor the boat in a good position, cover the sails and prepare the berth for the night. All this under the eyes of a middle-aged man who from the moment I'd cast the anchor into the mud of the marina had turned the spectacle of my arrival into his entertainment. At the time, it was fairly common to find vacationers or bored villa owners hanging about in our ports. For them, the arrival of an unknown craft, whether rowboat or dredger, was enough to dispel the melancholy of their stay on a lake. They might have come seeking pleasure and relaxation, but they ended up dealing with all manner of hassle if they were property owners, or being ripped off by hoteliers if they were just tourists. Toward evening, all of them found themselves longing for the seaside, where they could have gone around between the bunkers and recently dismantled block-houses gorging on naked women, fried fish, dances and films.

Leaning against the iron bar of the railing like a ship's captain, the man watching me from above the quay didn't actually fit any of those categories of lakeside malcontents, who realize too late that they've made the wrong choice. He had the air of someone with a fondness for the place, and he was enjoying the silence around him. The little houses along the shore, the restaurant, the tobbaconist's and the sailing shop—always closed—were so devoid of life, movement of people or goods, they looked as if they'd been painted on canvas.

Behind the houses a wall of laurel, magnolias, pines, acacias, camphor, and a bit farther up, chestnuts and oaks hung over the water where I was busying myself, turning it green and dark like the bottom of a pond.

Still under the calm and watchful eye of that landlubber standing against the railing, I pulled the waterproof tarpaulin over the boat, covering it for the night. Then I pulled hard on the mooring rope to align the stern with the quayside. I let go of the rope and with one leap, I was on land.

When I got to the top of the granite stairway that led to the pier, I found myself so close to the sole witness to my arrival that it was natural for us to greet each other with a nod and a quiet "Good evening," the way you do out of courtesy and good manners with people you don't know in the mountains, at sea or on the water, at any rate, when you're traveling and you meet other travelers.

I was already headed toward the Ristorante Vittoria when I heard the question: "Excuse me, may I ask you something?"

I turned. "Of course," I replied.

Without the least sign of flippancy, the man inquired, "What sort of boat do you have? Is it a brig, a barquentine, a sloop or a schooner?"

It wasn't the first time I'd been asked something like that in these lakeside ports. My boat actually had the solid appearance of a whaler or a bragozzo, and couldn't be categorized in the recognized tonnage.

"It's a yacht with a jib and a square-top mainsail," I replied. "It was designed and built before the war by the engineer Vittorio Quaglino, from Intra. He conceived it for sea-fishing and hoped to build a series. It's not pretty, but it's roomy, comfortable and easy to manage—to the extent that I can control it on my own. It has a little kitchen and two couchettes inside."

Not entirely satisfied, this respectable but curious fellow then asked why my boat was called *Tinca*; he'd read it on the transom.

"Maybe because it's squat and potbellied like the tench fish," I answered. "And it's the name Quaglino gave it. It's not to my taste, but I'm used to it. I could have thought of a better one—I'd have liked *Tortuga*, but changing the name of a boat or ship seems to bring bad luck."

"You don't fish?" he asked again. He positioned himself between me and the village.

"No, I don't. I follow the wind around the lake. At night,

I stop in one of these little ports, take a short walk, go and eat in a hotel. Then I come back to the boat and sleep below deck—or if it's hot, on deck, protected by the canvas."

"What a life!" he remarked. By now more interested in me than in my boat, he offered me a drink in a cafe in front of us, a local serving sodas and ice cream, and selling punches or perhaps a little grappa during the winter when a few travelers wait there, chilled, for the morning boats to arrive or depart.

He made as if to sit down on one of the straw chairs outside the cafe, and introduced himself: "Orimbelli."

I, too, said my surname in a hurry. And then I sat beside him in front of the lake, which was now in shadow. We were like two old acquaintances from the village who spend the dinner hour in company with little to say, simply watching the world go by together.

"Your health," he said, raising his *aperitivo*.

"And yours." I looked at him. He drank with his eyes on the glass and his face intent, like a priest after the offertory. He was about forty, rather small, sturdy, with a large neck. His short, pear-shaped head was covered with a growth of dark, thinning hair brushed carefully to spread it out. He looked Japanese, or Mongolian; the corners of his almond-shaped eyes turned down. They were an indefinable color, and different from each other in expression, so that it seemed as if he was squinting even when he wasn't. He smiled often, sometimes for no reason, as if to seem obliging, but with the world-weariness of a gentleman, or a man who's lived a lot. His voice was somewhat nasal and yet not the least bit affected. He wore a gold ring on his little finger, and a fancy wristwatch, the kind that tells the day and month as well as the hour.

It was immediately obvious that he was someone of a certain refinement, but it wasn't easy to pin down his class. Clearly, he wasn't a businessman or industrialist. Perhaps a doctor, a notary, or just a rich idler who had established himself by the lake before the war, someone who'd only stuck his head out after the army had gone by, to see which way the wind was blowing.

To satisfy my curiosity, which was growing faster than his, I started talking a bit more about my boat and myself, in the hope that he'd exchange some of his own confidences.

"The boat's good," I continued, "for getting around, going from port to port. I stop off at the islands, get out sometimes at the Castelli di Cannero. I dock under the cliff at Santa Caterina or in old, abandoned ports such as Sasso Carmine or Gabella di Maccagno. Every now and then I go back to my home port at Luino, where I have a house."

He listened, but he clearly didn't know the lake that well, since the names of these places didn't mean much to him.

I started up again. "I go here and there to pass the time, occasionally with a girl or a friend. I came back here a year ago from Switzerland. I was interned there from '43 to '45."

"Me, too," he interrupted. "I got back a year ago from the war. Or should I say, the place I ended up in on account of the war."

I realized I'd finally triggered something in him. Pretty soon I'd know everything there was to know about him.

"I've come back from Puglia," he said, "or rather Naples, where I was waiting for north Italy to be liberated so I could return to my wife's family in Milan. I parted from them in '36 when I left for the campaign in Ethiopia. I never imagined things would last so long."

"But in October of '36 the war in Africa was already over," I observed.

"Of course it was," he replied. "But I had to stay. I was detained. In '41, I came back to Italy so as not to end up a prisoner of the English. I stayed in Naples to improve my health. I'd gotten an amoeba in Africa. A Puglian official I knew at the military hospital invited me to stay with him. A day goes by, then a month—you know how life is—what with one thing and another, the Allies landed. I had to wait. I went back to Naples, where I got into business in order to make a living, and after that I stayed for a while in Rome. Finally last year, after the liberation, I came back to Milan. My wife had been evacuated here to our villa. I rejoined her, and I've been here on the lake for about a year now. We don't have children, and we get a bit bored. It's possible we'll go back to Milan for the winter."

He'd recounted half his life story to me without my getting a handle on him. There was the fact of his having been living away from his wife, perhaps not totally involuntarily. I dismissed the idea of his being an adventurer, a globe-trotter or a chancer—he had the air of being a serious person, grounded and reflective. What's more, he had a villa, one of the ones that overlook the lake from the promontories nearby, where he surely lived on independent means, like the lord he seemed the moment I spotted him as I entered the port.

"Are you dining at the Vittoria this evening?" he asked me.

"Yes," I said. "I know Cavallini, who runs the place. I came here in '42 before decamping to Switzerland. It was one of the few places that managed to put on a real spread despite the war and the risk of prison."

"Was life hard here in those years?" he asked.

"Hard for those who didn't know how to work around things. But with a bit of effort you could find anything. The butchers killed calves in the woods and at night the bakers made rolls and small baguettes with white flour. You could get coffee, too. I think butter and rice were exported over the mountains to Switzerland—contraband stuff, since they had rationing there as well. You had to turn a blind eye to the prices, that's for sure!"

"Well, tough times," he concluded.

"Tough times," I agreed.

"But how was it as an internee in Switzerland?" he began again.

"Depended. Those with money had a certain freedom and did all right. But those without it went to labor camps. If they weren't able to work, they went to nursing homes, which were like asylums, but had the basics."

"Listen," he interrupted me, convinced I'd been one of those with money in Switzerland, "might I have the pleasure of inviting you to dine with me at the villa? You won't eat as you would at Cavallini's, but we can chat a bit. It happens so rarely in this village! I'll just run up to let the staff know—and my wife, of course."

He didn't even give me time to make polite noises, but got up and went toward the villa. He walked quickly but calmly, his trousers a bit loose at the back as if they'd been cut badly or made before he went to Ethiopia, and after ten years were now too large. I wondered if he were not a former career officer, one of those colonels who, once discharged, don't wear civilian clothes very well anymore.

Ten minutes later he was back. Whatever difficulties he might have had, he'd emerged victorious from the battle with his wife or staff, because he invited me to follow him.

The villa was a few minutes from the road, concealed within lush gardens. On one of the pillars of the gate I read the words VILLA CLEOFE written in black.

He took me around the grounds before introducing me to his wife. I noticed that the estate had a harbor with a small dock to the side. I stopped to study the layout and size it up. Orimbelli must have understood the reason for my interest. As if responding to a request I hadn't dared to make, he said, "Of course, if you pass by here and want to dock your boat, please go ahead. It's empty."

At last he let me cross the threshold. The door, under a glass roof with a border of lacy, perforated metal, faced the road. Inside, the hallway was hung with prints, and three doors led off to right and to left. At the end was the first flight of stairs, with a red carpet-runner such as you'd see in a hotel. Between the banister and the wall, in shadows barely touched by the light coming through a blue and red glass panel, you could make out a bronze statue on a pedestal of black marble: a shepherdess with a basket over her arm.

Orimbelli opened the first door on the right and led me into the drawing room, which was almost dark. Seated on a sofa in the dim light coming from the garden were two women.

"My wife," he said, indicating the first one.

I bowed deeply.

He then indicated the second, much younger than the first. "My sister-in-law, Matilde Scrosati, widow of the late Berlusconi."

I bowed no less deeply, acknowledging her widowhood. It must have been recent since she was wearing a black chiffon dress.

"As I told you, this man owns a fine cutter that arrived in port only an hour ago," Orimbelli explained to the women.

They nodded with faint smiles.

"He's a sportsman. A sailor who tours the lake on his own for pleasure."

"From Milan?" asked Signora Orimbelli.

"No," I replied, "I'm from the lake area, or at least I was born here . . ."

The conversation didn't appear to be taking off. Fortunately the door opened, and a housekeeper in a white apron appeared. Dinner was served. Behind the maid, you could see that the table had been prepared in the dining room.

All the lights were on even though it wasn't yet evening, so I could observe the two women at table while the old maid slowly served us. A fine risotto came first, then a mixed grill, followed by salad, cheese, fruit and coffee. Orimbelli served wine to me and to himself; the women drank water.

Across from me, Signora Ormibelli was very thin, schoolmarmish and snooty. She was at least ten years older than her husband, with a dry, creased face and graying hair parted down the middle. Her body was straight and neat like a man's. Between bites, she silently watched first me and then her husband, trying to work out why he'd brought me to the house, perhaps suspecting that we were up to something—that the casual meeting at the port was just a pretext concocted by her husband for offering shelter to one of his unsavory companions from Africa or Naples.

For her part, the sister-in-law, widow of the signora's brother, seemed pleased to have company at table. She was young, voluptuous, pale and blond, with huge, innocent eyes. She seemed a little flabby but she held herself well, and two formidable breasts protruded from beneath the chiffon veil that enveloped her. An ill-fitting bra squeezed them into melons, but without it they'd surely have been more pendulous, like pears. Whenever she straightened up to drink or take a breath, they got in her way.

A magnolia flower, I thought. A lush, delicate tuberose,

with who knows what hidden roots. A bit listless, maybe, with a bittersweet mouth and a cowed gaze, probably the result of dreaminess or else faux timidity. After the cruel and premature loss of the only man who'd ever touched her, someone who was irreplaceable, other men must have seemed like enemies. Hidden behind mourning veils and squeezed into invisible lingerie, she sat next to her sister-in-law like a daughter, her attitude respectful and secure. It was perfectly clear that as long as she was next to the scowling, upright Signora Cleofe, her beauty would, unfortunately, never get her into trouble.

Orimbelli didn't even bother to glance at her. When he did speak of her, nodding toward her without looking over, both out of respect for a guest and in an attempt to make amends for the women's ungracious silence, it was to tell me that Signora Matilde could be considered a war widow. Her husband had disappeared during the battle of Lake Ascianghi. "Disappeared" was a polite euphemism used to indicate "unrecovered" or "unrecognized," just as so many others who'd been hit by grenades or artillery bullets.

The widow ate quietly, as if her brother-in-law were talking about things that didn't concern her—or things she'd already heard too often. Now and again she looked at her sister-in-law beside her, who actually seemed angered by the discussion. Only toward the end of lunch did she glance at me to ask, "Coffee?"

During coffee, which was served by a young woman who hadn't appeared before, Signora Orimbelli spoke—revealing yellowed teeth—in order to complete or correct some of the information her husband thought he'd given me.

"Yes," she said, her neck stiffening like a turkey's, "we spent ten years on our own, from '41 in Milan and then the last five years here in this villa. It was my father's; it's now mine. This man here was away, in Puglia, Naples and who knows where else. My brother Angelo, poor thing, never came back—he disappeared down there, or died. Nothing was ever known about it. If he were still of this world, he'd have shown up by now."

Orimbelli kept silent. He lit a cigar and smoked it silently, his gaze wandering between the ceiling and the table.

I deemed it the right moment to take my leave. Orimbelli wanted to go with me as far as the port but I wouldn't let him. Promising to return soon, I followed the main road. At the time, few cars used it, especially at night.

The *Tinca* was waiting for me, unmoving, in the still waters of the harbor. I slipped under the canvas without even lighting the kerosene lamp, and five minutes later I was asleep.

The next day I hoisted the sails before eight. I glided past the Villa Cleofe on my way to the open water, and noticed that all the windows on the lake side were still shut.

Who knows how often I'd sailed past that villa in my boat without noticing it, just as I'd gone past so many others, both large and small, surrounded by grounds that overlooked the lake on one shore or the other? Grand old houses, their gardens lush with greenery, their docks covered in wisteria or woodbine. All of them facing the lake, most of them shut up, silent. *Think of all those love affairs*, I mused, *everything that goes on behind those stately facades.* And I tacked, in order to catch the first breath of the *tramontana*, the cold north wind coming off the promontory at Cannero.

II

FOR FIVE DAYS I resisted the temptation to return to Oggebbio, where it seemed I'd scented one of the lake's many hidden mysteries. But one afternoon, while I was on my way back to my home port, I moved out of the wind so I could pass within sight of the villa. I was three hundred meters offshore and moving beyond it when I noticed a signal from the terrace. Someone was waving a towel, or a large white handkerchief. I drew up and recognized Orimbelli on the lookout. There was nothing for me to do but lower the sails and coast into his dock.

"I spotted you half an hour ago with my binoculars when you were abreast of Laveno," he said from the edge of the terrace. "Come on in. You're in time for tea."

The two women were in fact taking tea under the great copper beech that stood on the shady side of the villa. Matilde was serving, and she had the vague air of being happy to see me again. After tea, she was anxious to go down to the dock to inspect my boat with her brother-in-law. I showed them everything, from the rigging to the couchettes, even the little toilet I'd fixed up under the prow.

"A veritable yacht!" Orimbelli exclaimed. "And to live on it, as you do, all summer long . . . "

"A tub," I said with false modesty. "Not much more than a rowboat or fishing boat."

It was understood that I'd stay for supper. Even the old serving maid, Lena, nicknamed Lenin, welcomed me with a lovely smile. I realized that my presence was actually necessary in order to breathe some fresh air into that atmosphere, and to make Signora Cleofe bearable. I noticed later that she retracted her claws only when I was around. Not only did she retract them, she sought to convince me that she didn't have any, that she was a wounded spirit, aggrieved, yet full of resignation and tolerance.

A young man like me, in his thirties, free and well-off, if I really did have a yacht, one of only two or three of all the boats on the lake at that time . . . A serious person (and by now she was convinced I must be), who would go back to work in some bank or family business after the holidays. It was clear she didn't dislike me at all, even if my way of life was somewhat perplexing. She went as far as asking me openly what sort of work I did.

"So, are you in industry or business? Or maybe you're a professional, an engineer, perhaps, like my poor brother?"

"To tell you the truth, I don't have any employment at the moment," I replied. "Last summer I came back from Switzerland, where I was a refugee, as your husband will have told you. I'm still looking around for something to do, something suitable . . . "

"If you wait much longer," she retorted tactlessly, "you'll end up like my husband. At forty he has yet to discover what work suits him."

So as not to disenchant her, I invented a story on the spot, telling her that come autumn I would begin work with a friend, a furrier and importer of hides. I'd end up in the leather business, a few days in the Milan office and a few at the tannery at Verolanuova in the province of Brescia. But I didn't have any pressing need to earn, since I was from a good family and wasn't—how could I put it?—exactly penniless. I explained. "I've got some little places inherited from my uncle, houses I'm going to renovate which rent fairly well."

Matilde was watching me unobtrusively. She'd changed for dinner, and had put on an iron-gray dress over a puffy, rose-colored blouse that ballooned over her bosom, making it look like an enormous carnation.

Taking advantage of his wife's exceptionally good mood, Orimbelli talked about the war in Africa. It seemed to obsess him. He'd been an officer in the Somalian mounted squadron under General Aimone Cat, had fought with honor and made a victorious entry at Gondar. His brother-in-law had also been at the front during one of the counterattacks that decided the war in the Lake Ascianghi region, but he hadn't been seen or heard from since the 2nd of April 1936. Orimbelli passed over his brother-in-law to talk about the marches and the battles, about Addis Ababa, Badoglio and Graziani, but above all about Aimone Cat, who'd recommended him for a silver medal. It came to nothing, however, when it was discovered that Orimbelli was not an enlisted member of the Fascist party.

During the discussion, it emerged that three months ago, they'd begun the process of filing papers at the Court of Assizes in Milan to have the poor engineer, Angelo, declared "presumed dead." The requisite ten years had passed since he'd last been heard from alive.

"We were married by proxy at the end of November '35," said Matilde, shaking her head.

Signora Cleofe gave her a severe look, perhaps to shut her up on a subject unsuitable for discussion with strangers.

"By proxy?" I asked.

"Yes, by proxy," Matilde went on, indifferent to her sister-in-law's glare. "Poor man! It seemed he knew he wouldn't be back. We should have been married before he left, but the papers weren't ready, so our marriage was celebrated in absentia. He presented himself to the bishop of Asmara and four weeks later, when the papers came from Milan, I went to get married in my own parish. My husband's proxy, Professor Ernesto Configliacchi, put the ring on my finger. He was my husband's professor from the polytechnic. You'll have heard of him as he's a celebrated man."

"Of course!" I responded. "Who hasn't heard of Professor Configliacchi!" even though the name was new to me, and faintly ridiculous. "So are you legally a widow?" I continued.

Orimbelli interrupted. "What does it matter? Proxy marriages become invalid if they're not consummated within six months, and after six months he was no more . . . She's wanted to consider herself married these ten years," he nodded knowingly at Matilde, "out of devotion to the memory of the missing. But my wife has presented the application, and with the declaration of 'missing, presumed dead,' she'll come into possession of the whole of the inheritance, which her father left undivided. As it should be, if you like."

"If you like, and even if you don't, Mr. Lawyer!" his wife pointed out. When her husband had said he was a lawyer, or rather, a law graduate, she responded to the line with, "Graduate in law, or rather in nothing, since if a law graduate doesn't practice as a lawyer or a notary, what good is the degree? It's a piece of paper, an excuse for saying: I've made the effort, and now I have the right to take it easy for the rest of my life."

That's how I got involved in their affairs that night, and when Orimbelli suggested I should sleep in the house, his wife showed not the least surprise.

"Of course!" she said. "You wouldn't want to send him to sleep in his boat in the dock!"

"Then let's put him in the bishop's room," he said. The evening ended with a Chartreuse, and he took me up to the first floor. He opened the third door on the right, turned on the light and ushered me into a room carpeted in red, with a canopy of gold-painted wood hanging from the ceiling. From the canopy and around the bed hung brocade curtains, the same red as the carpet. At the foot of the bed was a white trunk framed in metal. On its rounded lid the letters T.M.O. could be seen stamped in black.

"The bishop?" I asked, indicating the three letters.

"No, it's my trunk. It's gone everywhere with me since I went to university. It's been all over Europe, and of course to Africa. My name is Temistocle Mario Orimbelli," he said, pointing to the initials.

"And the bishop? How does he come into it?"

"Monsignor Alemanno Berlusconi, the bishop, was my wife's great-uncle. He died in '28, and until twenty years ago, he spent summers at this villa. My wife's father decorated the best room for him in the manner suited to a prelate who'd been a papal legate in various parts of the world and part of the Congregation of Rights. At the time I wasn't around to know him, but Cleofe remembers him well. As you can see, his prayer stool is still there, beside the bed. And here: look . . ."

He went over to the large wardrobe and opened it. Up high, on a hanger, was a bishop's cassock in red cloth, with buttons right down to the hem and an amice over the shoulders. Over the crook of the hanger you could see the skullcap positioned where the head might have been. Placed neatly together on the floor of the wardrobe below the vestments was a small pair of shriveled black shoes, the silver of the buckles so faded it looked like lead. Despite the odor of naphthalene issuing from the wardrobe, the bishop's clothing seemed fairly moth-eaten.

Orimbelli closed the doors again with a satisfied smile.

He then opened a little door beside the bed which was concealed by a curtain. I hadn't noticed it before.

"The comfort room."

I looked in, spotted a sink and imagined the rest.

With the air of having completed his duties as head of the house, my host made as if to retire discreetly. I said good night, thanked him and closed the door.

Then, suspicious of the trunk—it seemed I'd heard a thud from within—I tried to open it, but found it secured with three locks and a padlock. So I opened the wardrobe again and looked at the bishop's clothing. It was from there that the sound had come: beside the shoes, I spotted a sack of mothballs that must have fallen from within the vestments when the door was closed a few moments before.

III
—

IN THE MORNING, I set sail around eight as usual. Orimbelli
and I breakfasted together before he went up to the terrace to
wave me off. The two women were still in bed.

It seemed a shame to be leaving there after such a deli-
cious sleep in the bishop's bedroom. I felt strongly that I was
a part of that strange family after only two visits.

Orimbelli yelled from the terrace above. "Remember
your promise! You're coming back the day after tomorrow!"

Two days went by. After a stop at Ascona, where I had a girlfriend, I returned to Oggebbio. I hugged the shore, a morning tramontana on my right. Only a week before, that wind
would have taken me all the way to the islands. I arrived at
midday, which pleased Orimbelli; he'd thought I wouldn't
get there until evening.

The meal, served by Lenin, found us all in great spirits,
apart from Signora Cleofe, who was suffering an attack of trigeminal neuralgia. It was an illness she'd put up with inter-
mittently for years, and for which she'd found no remedy.

I asked who it could be in the kitchen, producing such

exquisite and beautiful dishes. I thought Matilde might at least have inspired them. But I actually learned from her that Martina was the cook. She was the daughter of Lenin and Domenico, the gardener: a family of three serving another of three. Domenico, Lenin and Martina lived in the little gatekeeper's lodge on the main road beside the entrance.

Orimbelli could hardly have done better than this. You could see why he felt no desire to return to Milan and do any old job. At the villa, he had a soft bed, good food, balmy air, peace and comfort. Perhaps all that was missing was a woman or two, given that his wife was obviously out of the question. After the ten-year break in marital relations, she was officially off-limits, he'd confided in me that morning. He'd then asked discreetly how the visit to my friend at Ascona had gone.

But his wife was the last person anyone would have taken account of. If you'd wanted to divine the secrets of the villa, you'd have had to consider Matilde, or possibly Martina, who was a large woman in her thirties—so long as you could, within those walls, escape the notice or suspicions of Signora Cleofe. And always supposing you could apply the usual rules to Orimbelli, and such a gentleman could be thought to want something more than rest and relaxation after such an adventurous life. That long, unbroken rest discharged soldiers seemed to long for as balm for their hidden injuries—a welcome daze, within which to conceal themselves for the rest of their lives.

•

At coffee after lunch, I turned to the *ammazzacaffè*, the little glass of grappa. Orimbelli asked if I'd be willing to take him on a short sailing trip—just for a couple of hours, so he could see what sailing had to recommend it.

It could be that he came up with the idea of trying out the *Tinca* in order to detain me, to keep me around, eating and sleeping with them at the villa.

That afternoon I took him on board. He'd never set foot on a sailing boat, but he found his feet perfectly. In less than an hour, he'd learned to let out the jib and fix it to the other side as we tacked. I even let him stay at the helm for a bit with the crosswind, so he could get a feel for the boat. I held to the inverna and covered the triangle between Oggebbio, Caldé and Ghiffa, letting him try some fast runs at the stern and sailing between Ghiffa and Oggebbio. After a couple of crossings he was full of enthusiasm. He actually asked if I'd take him aboard as a cabin boy starting the next morning.

When Signora Cleofe heard that evening that her husband was playing sailor, she was almost happy. "At least he'll get out of here," she said with a sigh of relief.

Orimbelli was up by seven. He'd taken some woolen vests from his wardrobe, shorts, tennis shoes, a sailing jacket, jumpers, bathing trunks (somewhat old-fashioned) and a white safari jacket, and slung his Zeiss binoculars across his shoulders. I advised him to take along a suitcase packed with a suit, a few shirts and a tie, since we'd be away for three days and might end up lunching in a hotel.

He took his place at the prow between the rigging, ready to work the jib. He didn't even ask me where I was headed. The wind was blowing from the north as it did every morning. I decided to catch it, and patiently, tack by tack, we passed the Castelli di Cannero, islets in the middle of the lake. By midday we docked the *Tinca* in the little port of Sasso Carmine, where I knew a good *osteria*. During lunch, we agreed to sail into the Swiss part of the lake. By the afternoon, the tailwind, the inverna, would have died down; already we could see the signs in the small clouds blowing across the crest of the mountains.

Before the wind fell we made it through border control, with its temporary import rules for the craft at Poggio Valmara, and were in the port of Ascona.

Sailing comfortably with the wind behind us, I confided in him that the girl in Ascona whom I'd spoken about, Charlotte, was actually the wife of a physics professor at Aarau. She was spending a month in one of their vacation apartments while her husband was in England doing some research in a large laboratory.

"I'm a man of the world," he said, "and I understand these things perfectly well."

So I suggested, "I might stay overnight in her apartment. If I do, would it bother you to sleep on your own in the boat?"

"Excuse me," he answered, "you're asking an old veteran of the African wars? I've slept under the stars countless times!"

•

Things turned out differently, because Charlotte had a friend from Berne staying with her, and Germaine rather liked Orimbelli.

All of us ate together in a restaurant at the port before going back to the apartment to drink and listen to American records. Orimbelli must have been a great dancer in his day: he danced all the numbers with Germaine, frequently going out onto the terrace to whirl around in the dark.

"What a shame!" he said, coming back into the room after one of these exits. "Germaine goes back to the Swiss mainland tomorrow! She's really nice and so interesting."

Germaine was about twenty-five, and the crème de la crème as far as women go. She was bubbly and determined to take advantage of her youth and beauty, at least during the holidays. I suggested she put off her departure for one more day so we could enjoy her company a bit longer, and she agreed. She and Charlotte could accompany us in the boat as far as Stresa, where she could get the Orient Express to Briga and from Briga, a direct train to Berne.

When everything was arranged, I got ready to retire with Charlotte. I wished Orimbelli good night and asked him to be sure the mooring was secure when he went to sleep at the port.

"So," I said, "everyone in the boat at nine tomorrow morning!"

But when I went to the kitchen next morning to make a coffee, I found him in the hallway in his underwear. He stood there like a thief caught in the act, his head lowered, shoulders hanging.

"The flesh is weak!" he said.

I cheered him up, saying it wasn't weakness but strength, and that one wouldn't have expected less from an old veteran of the African war, like him. He went back into Germaine's room feeling brighter.

At nine all four of us were at the port ready to set sail; Orimbelli had carried his friend's heavy suitcase for her.

"Faithful friends! To the islands!"

The women were happy since they'd never been to the Borromean Islands. We were able to get to customs at Poggio Valmara on the last puff of the tramontana. After the formalities, we sailed slowly toward Maccagno, waiting for the inverna. As soon as we were in the open and out of sight of the Guardie di Finanza, the women took off their clothes to get an all-over tan. They came and went from below deck where they were making lunch, so we got a good front and rear view.

Orimbelli was beaming from his seat at the foot of the mast. "Wow, this is crazy! This is the life! Bliss!"

Halfway across the lake, a rare wind—the *munscendrin*-took us by surprise. Every two or three years, it comes up from the glaciers hidden behind the Levantina Valley in the Ceneri Mountains, and blows southward.

By this time Orimbelli felt he was an expert on winds and he queried my identification. "It's the tramontana," he said. "Nothing but the tramontana."

In any case it was a favorable wind, and we used it to sail on, dropping anchor between the two Castelli di Cannero a little after midday. There was no one around, and we disembarked for a picnic lunch with our naked Swiss women, to whoops of enthusiasm from Orimbelli. He was white as a plucked chicken in his swimming trunks, jumping over the grass, getting into the water and trying to climb up walls, while the women started a fire under a spit. The smell of roasting brought him back to the group quickly, and with his hearty appetite, he was the first to start eating.

He held his cutlet by the bone like a barbarian and bit into it. "It's been nearly a year since I've eaten meat." And he winked and nodded at Germaine, who was leaning against his side, dangling a Swiss sausage—a white one, made of veal, bratwurst—between her teeth.

"Don't tell me you don't know a thing or two where women are concerned," I said to him.

"Believe me, no," he declared, and he stopped chewing. "Since I came back from the south, I've practically fasted. I'm not saying it was like that before. On the contrary! But at Oggebbio, with my wife constantly watching me? Can you believe, she's even forbidden Martina, the gardener's daughter, to clean my room! Lenin tidies it. My wife has always considered me a weakling, someone who sees a woman and loses his head . . . She's jealous, obsessed and convinced that all women fall at my feet. A good thing you arrived to set me free! Long live the *Tinca*!" And he winked again to show me what he meant by *tinca*.

Sitting on the grass beside me a little later, he told me that following the arrival of some anonymous letters from Naples, she'd initially persuaded herself that he'd got a second family down there, complete with wife and children. Then she'd ended up thinking he was keeping a young lover in a little flat at Intra where he'd visit her once a week. And all this was based on the fact that now and again he went to Intra to buy things such as tobacco, illustrated papers and some books.

"Complete fabrications," he said. "But I'm not saying I haven't been well loved in my life. Sometimes when I think about the love of which I've been, and actually still am the object, I realize I couldn't live without this kind of nourishment. Do you know the salamander?"

"Of course I do—the little yellow and black crocodile-like animal that appears on paths after rain."

"Right. I've studied the salamander, and it's an animal that needs water almost more than the fish do. Try catching one and putting it in the garden. It'll die, all dried up. In order to live it needs to stay in the water, in brooks or streams. If you keep it in the garden, it shrivels up, goes flat, loses its color and dies in no time. Without love—and I mean love, not sex—I'm like a salamander on land."

He winked again at Germaine, who was speaking German with Charlotte.

"It's not that I'd turn down a gift from God," he added, "but I can do without certain things if I have to. Without love, no."

IV
—

THE INVERNA WAS RISING, and in the clear watery mirror in the middle of the lake, between Laveno and Intra, a big dark blot could be seen approaching from the south. It was the usual afternoon wind, low and tense, rippling the water without stirring it up, and touching it with myriad points of light.

The *Tinca* wasn't made for sailing close-hauled, against the wind, but we were aiming for Stresa and we needed to leave. With three wide tacks the prow was approaching Oggebbio.

Orimbelli pointed his binoculars at Villa Cleofe. "I don't see anyone, but maybe it would be a good idea to ask the women to go below deck. There aren't any other binoculars at home, but we're getting a bit too close, and Cavallini is always on the lookout."

I agreed. "Yes, and if we want to skirt the tip of Laveno with a single tack, we'll have to get pretty close to land."

"We're passing close to the town our friend lives in," I told the two women. "It'd be better if you two went down to take a nap."

They wondered if they couldn't just put on their swimsuits, but I persuaded them to make themselves scarce. I turned at the dock at Villa Cleofe, about thirty meters from the wall.

When we'd sailed almost as far as the fort at Cerro in the Gulf of Laveno, I cried out, "Sailors on deck!" Charlotte and Germaine emerged, now dressed, and spied the Borromean archipelago, its profile silhouetted against the Ossola Valleys.

We stopped first at Isola Bella and then Isola Pescatori, and at sunset we went to drop anchor in the port of Stresa. We had to say good-bye to Germaine that night since she was returning to Berne, so we marked the occasion by booking two large rooms at the Hotel des Iles Borromées and dining like royalty in the restaurant.

The next day we were at the station around ten. Germaine wouldn't stop talking about how short her stay in Stresa had been, and how she'd liked the room she'd spent the night in. "This morning when I opened the balcony windows and saw the lake colored like mother-of-pearl and the fog-bound islands slowly taking shape as they do in a Chinese or Japanese watercolor, it seemed like a dream . . ."

Orimbelli, finding himself omitted from the list, didn't think much of his friend's romantic description of the marvels of the place. He stood on the pavement in his white safari jacket, holding his linen hat and looking melancholy, and waiting for the kiss Germaine blew to him at last from the train when it started moving.

"Take heart!" I said to him as soon as the Orient Express had gone. "For each one who leaves, ten more arrive."

"Isn't that the truth!" he exclaimed, and all at once he perked up.

You could do anything with this fellow. So I decided to play a trick on him.

During our midday meal in a waterfront restaurant, I went to the telephone several times, explaining that I was working on a deal and had to follow it through. When I came back to the table the second time, I told him I'd unfortunately have to go to Milan that afternoon to meet some people for dinner so I could wrap the matter up the following morning. I was sure to be back by noon the next day.

When it was just him and me, I said, "I'll leave the *Tinca* and Charlotte in your care. Keep an eye on the boat and keep the lady company. You're a gentleman, and I'd trust you with my life."

"Don't mention it!" he exclaimed. "I'm a soldier and I know the meaning of friendship and loyalty."

I didn't go to Milan but, as I'd arranged with the two phone calls I'd made in the restaurant, I took a boat instead to the Isola Pescatori to stay at the Albergo Verbano, where an acquaintance of mine from Milan was on vacation.

The following day I returned to Stresa on the first crossing, and went to knock at the door to Charlotte's room. She opened up to me in pajamas and pointed to Orimbelli, lying naked and asleep in the middle of the bed.

"At bedtime last night, he started begging me not to leave him alone . . . I ended up giving in to him. I hope you won't take it badly," she said.

"No, no. Certainly not!"

"Ok, then I'll wake him up and let's see what spin he'll put on it."

"No. Let him sleep. Let's pretend nothing happened. I'm going to breakfast and I'll wait for you downstairs."

On my way to the little salon where breakfast was served, I asked myself what pretty young women from good families could possibly see in Orimbelli. He was forty and looked fifty, with an egg-shaped body and short arms and legs. His teeth were crooked and he was beginning to go bald. Nor was he a poet or an actor. He didn't have aristocratic manners and in common with all former officers, he was barely chivalrous. And yet . . .

I came to the bitter conclusion that men often undervalue their rivals and that women see things differently. It's a bit like the Chinese—they can tell one another apart perfectly well and find one another more or less beautiful, even though they all look the same to us.

Around noon, as we were heading for Ascona, I asked Orimbelli how he'd spent the night.

"Very well," he replied. But he immediately became suspicious and looked at Charlotte, who was turning her face toward the lake in order not to give it away. He understood everything. Lowering his head, he said forlornly, "The flesh is weak!"

We'd gotten as far as Oggebbio, but we were in the middle of the lake. From a distance, I looked toward Villa Cleofe—indistinguishable between the white dots on the coast—and asked myself what this man could have been doing all those years, between Africa and Italy, wherever he'd set foot. And there, too, on the grounds of the villa, in the bishop's bedroom, the kitchen, the greenhouse, even at the dock. Orimbelli was surely one of those devils who stir things up wherever they go, who lack respect or a shred of principle, a well-mannered monster, a wolf in sheep's clothing.

I was banking on arriving at Ascona with the *montive*, the little winds that spring up from the valleys along the lake at nightfall, and die down close to the shore. In the meantime, we went with the last breath of the inverna—or rather with those mysterious breezes that come from who knows where, sudden small flurries that dimple a short stretch of the lake and then disappear, only to reappear a little later from another direction, like sprites or jesters. If you know how to catch them and keep an eye on the wind gauge, they're enough to keep the boat moving and gliding lightly through the water. An almost imperceptible rippling follows the stern, and is immediately reabsorbed by the still surface of the lake.

To catch these puffs, I'd fixed some strips of very thin gauze to the rigging, and higher up, some birds' feathers tied to a silk thread. It's a refinement, the hobby of someone who spends his days on the water, and it's almost a point of honor to be able to glide along without taking out the oars or starting the motor.

We got as far as Maccagno on these bare hints of wind, half an hour after the sun went down. We were about to skirt a section of the lake between Maccagno and Ronco Scigolino,

which may be the most sinister of the entire Verbano area—
that is, after the one opposite Feriolo, where they say a whole
town was submerged. That's where, at some point during the
night of January 8, 1896—it's never been possible to pinpoint
the time—twelve men sank in the Guardie di Finanza's tor-
pedo boat. And the lake has surrendered not a single beret.

I told Orimbelli the story just as a few light puffs arrived,
one after another. They seemed to be coming from the depths
of the lake; the air was so still, and the water as smooth and
shiny as marble.

"The souls of twelve sailors surely lie beneath us in the
seaweed at the bottom," I said.

At these words, Orimbelli begged me never to refer, now
or in the future, to tragic events—or even merely sad ones.
"It's not superstition," he said, though he made the supersti-
tious sign of the horns with his fingers in the direction of the
wreck. "It's a precaution. You never know. It's best never to
bring up or recall any ill-omened event, even one that happened long ago or far away."

Meanwhile, the light gusts and first fannings of the land
breezes brought us to the customs point. Having passed
through, we began to fly with the wind toward the lights of
Ascona.

The *Tinca* passed between the Brissago Islands and the
coast, slipped into the shadow of the mountains and then
dented a vast watery mirror silvered by the moon, which had
just come out behind Gambarogno. Silently, it entered the
little port at Ascona before midnight.

At my request, Orimbelli took Charlotte to her house. He then returned to the boat, which I'd meanwhile docked and prepared for the night. He smoked a cigar and stretched out on his couchette, but before going to sleep he wanted to make sure I wasn't put out by his behavior of the night before. Sufficiently reassured, he pulled the sheet up to his head and fell into a deep sleep, just like a soldier from Africa, broken by fatigue.

Maybe he wasn't a demon, I thought, but a poor man shaken up by the wars, someone who'd learned to take what life offered him from one moment to the next. One of those innocents who, providing they had them, would eat their own children if they were hungry, so convinced were they of their rightness—or rather, that the rules of right and wrong did not apply to them. I knew it wasn't easy for him—or me, for that matter—to be any other way, or to be better. In recent years, we'd seen the world overturned. Between combat and prison, escapes and rescues, it had changed in our hands, without giving us time to understand the simple truth, which was that, having been present at these events and taken part in them—sometimes against our will—we had been enriched rather than damaged. We were convinced, instead, that we'd been robbed of our best years, and when the war was over we wanted to reinvent our youth. We wanted to recover, to make the most of our physical strength and our continuing youth. But perhaps it was a bit late, and time now to do other things.

It must have been this deep, fellow feeling that bound

me to Orimbelli, and made me go on these forays around the lake with him.

It was during one of our stops at the Villa Cleofe that I tried to gather some information about him. These stops were made necessary by Orimbelli's having to present himself to the local and provincial authorities armed with his law degree in order to obtain the requisite permits for carrying out the work of enlarging the lodge. While he chased documents and applications between Intra and Novara, I went to see Cavallini, the owner of the Ristorante Vittoria, and drew out of him everything he knew about Orimbelli. Part of his life, at least, began to come clear.

I found out that he was the only child of an innkeeper from Milan who'd set him up to become a lawyer, or at least get a law degree, by offering his professors cheap meals. While still a student, the future graduate had begun taking handouts from his father, who must have earned plenty. The moment he turned twenty, he was darting through the streets of Milan in a red car. He turned up regularly at San Siro for race meetings and showed up in the brothels and whorehouses like someone with a season ticket. Raffish and greedy, he ended up charming the daughter of a wealthy silk merchant as soon as he'd completed his degree. He married her believing he'd be able to squander her fortune, but he soon realized he wasn't going to fleece her so easily. Disillusioned, he volunteered for the war in Africa, and returned ten years later telling a string of yarns. As it happened, he'd lived in

Naples after Africa; he'd also been in prison there. Several months ago, he'd turned up in Oggebbio, fresh as a daisy, to live with his wife. But he was rumored to have a young lover in Intra, someone he'd brought with him from Naples.

"In prison for what?" I asked.

"Don't ask me that," Cavallini replied. "I don't want to speak ill of anyone. But they say that he was on the black market, and also a pimp."

"And how do you know all this?" I asked.

"A restaurant is like a seaport," he said. "Half the world passes through it, and if you know how to listen, you learn everything."

Cavallini had been a waiter for thirty years in London. He was a tall, fat man in his fifties with a big red face and curly black hair. He kept his wife in the kitchen, but he was always at the door of his restaurant, curious about everything and irritated by how little he was able to learn in a tiny place like Oggebbio. Still, his tentacles stretched over the whole of Verbano. There wasn't anything going on at Intra, Laveno or Cannobio that he didn't know about. He questioned all his clients, the boat captains and coach drivers, and made his own staff talk, too. And when he went shopping at Intra, he listened in cafes and at his suppliers.

Before I left, I asked him about the women at the Villa Cleofe.

"Real ladies, top-drawer people," he affirmed, raising his hand to vouch for the truth of what he was saying.

In fact, as if to confirm Signora Cleofe's social status,

her Puricelli cousins—known throughout Italy for the last fifty years as great manufacturers of hemp, linen and cotton—arrived that weekend for a visit from Milan: father, mother and two young girls. Signora Cleofe introduced me as a friend of her husband, a man of means and person of some standing, with a cutter at anchor in their dock. But it was easy to see how much weight a friend of Orimbelli had in the Puricellis' eyes. So little, in fact, that the next day, when the two girls shyly requested a spin in the boat, they met with Commendatore Puricelli's decisive refusal. Their mother had to intercede before the girls were permitted to board—and then for only half an hour, with my word that I'd stay within sight of the villa and not go more than a hundred meters beyond shore.

Irritated by having given in, Puricelli appropriated Orimbelli's Zeiss binoculars and sat on the terrace, his elbows resting on the railing. He focused on us with great attention, and not for nothing, because after a few minutes, he put down the binoculars and got to his feet, yelling and waving for us to come back. I got out the oars and immediately returned to the dock. Puricelli had come down to the little pier to wait for us, and he sent his daughters up to the house before rounding on me and asking why I'd made a lewd gesture; there could be no doubt about it, he'd seen it thanks to the binoculars.

I patiently explained that, offshore as we were, and without the slightest breath of air, I'd relied on an old method for testing whether the wind was blowing, and from which direction, a method that involved putting your index finger in your mouth, wetting it all over, and lifting it up. If it feels cold on one side, it means the wind is wafting from that direction. I told him that Orimbelli had copied the gesture on his own account, and the girls were curious, wanting to try feeling the wind for themselves a few times, like old boatswains.

Confounded, he looked as if he wanted to slap me.

"Try it yourself," I said to convince him.

He remained somewhat dubious. Then, determined, he put his finger in his mouth, took it out and raised it in the air. Orimbelli blew on his cousin's finger and asked him, "Do you feel the cold?"

"I feel it, I feel it," Puricelli responded through his teeth. "But what need was there for you to put your finger in the mouth of my Cristina?"

Orimbelli, who'd actually put his finger in the mouth of the elder sister, justified himself. "I was showing her how, just showing her how."

We returned to the terrace, where we found the two girls teaching their mother, Matilde and Signora Cleofe how to feel the wind on their fingers. Seeing the five women, one with her finger in her mouth and another with her finger in the air, Puricelli was overcome by a frightful rage. To put a stop to their game, he announced that he'd scheduled their departure for early the next morning.

V

AS SOON AS THE GRAND COUSINS HAD GONE, Orimbelli wanted to put out in the *Tinca*, despite the dead calm on the lake. To his annoyance, we could still see the villa after two hours. But the inverna, rising early, gathered us up before noon and carried us all the way to Ascona in one long run, almost always aft.

Orimbelli was anxious to get in touch with Germaine again. When she'd said good-bye a few days earlier, she'd let us know that one of her lovely friends would be arriving soon. I was less keen.

From a distance, I spied the *Lady*'s two masts standing tall against the dark foliage of the plants around the Castello. I went over to drop anchor in the small dock there. It was where Signor Kauffmann normally anchored. A Swiss German, he had the most beautiful boat you could see anywhere on Lake Maggiore, at Ascona. It so happened that our paths had crossed several times on the lake, and we'd exchanged the captain's greeting—a touch of the beret and a brief glance. I knew his base was Ascona, but I'd never found him at anchor there. He was always out sailing around the lake, and he often sheltered behind the long, tree-lined tongue of land that separated the basin of Ascona from that of Locarno. I never ventured there for fear of losing the winds.

I decided to visit him so I could get a close-up of his boat. It had to be a sort of Stradivarius, to judge by the way it behaved downwind. The jib and flying-jib, the mainsail and mizzen were fearlessly raised, secured by heaven knows how many quintals of lead in the keel and a draft that prevented the *Lady* from entering small ports and kept her offshore, swift and silent as *The Flying Dutchman*.

Orimbelli was completely ignorant about boats and barely glanced at the *Lady*, so I advised him to go off to town on foot, and said I'd join him after I docked the *Tinca*.

A true yachtsman, Signor Kauffmann showed me the *Lady*'s every detail. It was stunning. I saw some amazing electric capstans as well as gauges for wind and depth near the binnacle. Inside there were four couchettes with linen sheets, an electric kitchen and a bathroom with a shower.

In the central room, Kauffmann offered me an *aperitivo*, taking a bottle from a well-stocked bar.

Then, like a gentleman, he asked to come aboard the *Tinca*. He was good enough to find it pleasingly shaped, with well-proportioned sails considering its size. I was so touched I could have hugged him.

I went off happy, especially since he'd given me a small anchor with knotted arms that was too small for his boat. He couldn't use it, but it was heaven-sent for the *Tinca*, since it had been furnished with a clumsy old fisherman's anchor that was too heavy for it.

I slipped along the shore, grazing the plants that hung out over the water, and headed for port. Orimbelli had to be at one of the lakefront cafes, stretched out on one of those comfortable chairs foreigners lie on to take the sun at Ascona. I inspected the rows of tables, one after another, but didn't see him, so I sat outside in a cafe and waited for him to go by. All at once I heard his voice behind me. He was in a bar with a stranger, perhaps a Swiss German who spoke Italian. Their words filtered through to me from the open window I was sitting under.

"Did you say aconite?" Orimbelli was asking.

"Aconite," the other answered loudly, as if speaking to a deaf person. *"Aconitus napellus. Ja!* Is plant with huge roots. You take the drug from it. Extremely poisonous. *Ja.* Very poisonous! One milligram is enough to kill you."

"Die? How?" Orimbelli asked quietly.

"Central nervous system collapse," the German explained. "Muscular convulsions, cardiovascular paralysis. Then death!"

"And it's used as a drug?"

"Ja. Definitely," said the German, his voice louder and louder. "For trigeminal."

"For trigeminal neuralgia!" Orimbelli exclaimed. "Did you say for the trigeminal?"

"Ja, trigeminal, trigeminal, *tres gemìni,"* the other confirmed. "But only a tenth of a milligram!"

I called the waiter over so I could pay, and asked who those two talking in the cafe might be.

"One is a very famous professor at the University of Basel: Professor Kraus—he has a villa here in Ascona—and the other is an Italian who's buttonholed him."

I went to sit at a cafe a little farther along. Half an hour later I saw Orimbelli walk by.

"I've been exploring the center of the village, and I visited the Collegio Papio just as you suggested," he said as he sat down beside me. "Beautiful! I also visited the house of the painter Serodine, and the house where Carlo Borromeo slept four hundred years ago."

It was time to go to Charlotte's place. It was possible that she'd already seen the *Tinca* approaching the coast of Ascona a couple of hours ago from her apartment window.

Germaine's friend Hedwig had just arrived from Zurich. She was a single blonde in her thirties, tall and good-looking. The manager of a big shop on the Bahnhofstrasse, she was supremely elegant and set on marrying an Italian. She wanted him dark (but not from the south) and bilingual, with a degree. Or so Charlotte told us.

Hedwig came to Ticino three or four times a year to look around, but she never seemed to be able to find the right man.

Orimbelli boldly declared himself a bachelor. But he made the wrong moves from the start, no doubt paralyzed by Hedwig's exacting requirements. He began joking about the term "bilingual" and then gave Hedwig the once-over with the sort of greed women find terribly ill-mannered.

"She's amazingly *pizzuta*." He used a term he'd learned in Naples to refer to Hedwig's lush curves, which were actually rather surprising for someone so tall and thin. She was reminiscent of the female models in vogue during the Liberty period at the end of the nineteenth century.

Yet despite unpromising beginnings, the rapport between the two took a turn for the better that same day, and they went out together to shop for provisions for a three- or four-day cruise.

"Luckily she's rejected me as a husband," Orimbelli told me. "But it seems she's not opposed to me as a friend."

All the same, he had to sleep in the boat that night. Despite the drinking and dancing during the course of the afternoon and evening, both in the apartment and out on the terrace, the situation never lent itself to their getting it together the way it had with Germaine.

When I arrived at the port in the morning with the two women and our provisions, I found he'd got everything in order inside the boat. He was already hoisting the sails like a real sailor.

I took the helm. "What didn't happen last night will certainly happen during the voyage."

But it wasn't to be. Neither at the Castelli di Cannero nor at Baveno, where we stayed at the Hotel Suisse, could Orimbelli claim victory. Hedwig got as far as taking off her clothes on the boat, but she lay down at the prow protected by the bridge-house, insisting that "the men," as she called us, stay at the other end until the show was over.

"It's pointless," Orimbelli said. "There's nothing I can do. She's old, backward-looking, and she's Protestant—what's more, she's practicing. Maybe she's a lesbian, too."

At Meina we found only two double rooms, and he began to harbor some hope. He offered champagne and did miracles with his schoolboy French, and it suddenly seemed he'd succeeded in disappearing into one of the two rooms with Hedwig. But when I went to Charlotte's room with her, I found Hedwig there reading the *Zürcher Zeitung* while she waited for her friend. I had to retire to the other room, where Orimbelli was lying on one of the beds, fully clothed and extremely angry. I convinced him to get undressed and give up on the venture.

"When it's not happening, best not to insist," I said to him. "You'll see what catches we'll make over the next few days: a haul of women, such as shad and bass."

So as not to prolong his humiliation, I gave up on reaching Arona as I'd planned, and in a single day we sailed up the lake again to Ascona. I slept in the boat with him after we said good-bye to steely Hedwig and to Charlotte. She was expecting her husband to come back from England any day now.

VI

▬

"WHY DON'T WE LEAVE SWITZERLAND instead of hanging around here for nothing? Let's go and try our luck in our part of the lake. We'll be like St. Francis—when he discovered that the people where he was weren't ripe for conversion, he went back to Italy to harvest the people there, and not waste time and effort."

Orimbelli had a weakness for literary quotations, and another one for war stories; they always featured his old commander, Aimone Cat.

I also felt we'd do better to turn back to the Italian harvest, particularly since I'd been promising the two girls from Laveno a little cruise for some time.

The port of Laveno is in the middle of the city between the Ferrovie Nord train station and the town hall. It's in plain view of everyone, so exposed that the two girls didn't want to board the boat in such an open place. I had to wait an entire day before I could get them on board under cover of night. They arrived with their bags at just before midnight. Meanwhile Orimbelli, seated in a cafe near the port, patiently awaited our cargo. They were so frightened, so wary of being seen that I had to cast off and set out in the middle of the night. The montive wind had already fallen and in order to get us out of the gulf Orimbelli had to take to the oars, which were very heavy.

Once on the lake, we found the wind from a storm that had been rumbling for some time behind the Mottarone and was threatening to break out any moment. We'd agreed to cross the lake in order to shelter on the opposite shore when the thunderstorm suddenly broke. Torrents of water began falling, accompanied by squalls and flashes of lightning. Halfway across the lake, with the girls crouching below deck and shivering like leaves, Orimbelli let fear get the better of him, as if by contagion.

"What will we do if the boat capsizes?" he asked me.

"It doesn't capsize," I returned. "The *Tinca* is made for gales. The important thing is not to fall in the water. Keep your balance and steer cautiously."

One after another, bolts of lightening fell around the *Tinca*, which was floundering and rearing up like a horse now and again. The boat seemed static, almost chained to the bottom of the lake, and then it would run and fling itself toward the Piedmont shore, dipping now to the right, now to the left, depending on the blasts of wind and the waves that struck it.

Orimbelli stayed seated on deck, clinging mutely to the mast. By this stage he was incapable of manning the jib or carrying out any other maneuver. In the flashes of lightning I saw his face, white as the sail flapping around ominously and making almost more racket than the storm.

"One more kilometer," I said, "and we'll find a haven by the coast, where it's smooth as glass."

From below deck came the muffled cries of the girls. With every plunge, they feared the end had come, and began calling out for Mamma.

The fact was that an exceptionally strong current—the sort stirred up by a tempest—was drawing us toward the center of the lake. There, at the eye of the storm, there's no refuge whatever from the winds and, taking advantage of that limitless space, they let loose and raged to their heart's content.

I leaned toward Cannero to compensate for the leeward drift, seeking to bring us under the shelter of the mountains, but taking care not to turn the stern completely toward the storm for fear of heeling over.

The squalls were coming completely unexpectedly, because the dark kept you from seeing the cloudy water that accompanies them and gives some forewarning. But the boat held steady, heeding the rudder and the play of sails, and gradually gained ground toward the shelter of the coast.

All at once—as if by miracle—the wind fell and the lake grew calm. The sails slackened and the *Tinca* veered gently toward the shore. We'd passed the torrent at the center of the lake and entered the strip of coast protected by the Ghiffa promontory.

With everything in me, I bore up into the wind so as

not to crash into the shore, and the boat fell in line, calm as a tired horse.

Orimbelli revived. He groped around to unravel the cords he'd become tangled up in in the dark, and idly gave me a hand with the jib. He called out loudly to the girls, "Nothing to be afraid of! Come on up! The storm is over."

I beckoned for him to come closer. "Look over to the left," I said.

Only fifty meters away, the facade of Villa Cleofe could be seen through the last flashes of lightning, now distant. It stood out white against the dark backdrop of the trees.

"Shall we dock there?" I asked, bearing toward land.

"You've got to be kidding!" He begged me not to, his hands joined as if in prayer.

At that moment the light went on in the bishop's bed-room, and a shadow passed behind the window.

"My wife," Orimbelli said quietly. "She's heard the storm and is going around closing the shutters." And in fact, the light went out and a short time later came on again in another room.

"There's nothing for us to do but dock in the port at Oggebbio," I said. "If we keep going or turn back toward Intra, we'll end up in the middle of the wind again. We can't feel it here, but it's waiting for us less than a mile offshore, and who knows where it'll fling us."

"As long as you agree to lift anchor at dawn," he replied. "If Cavallini notices that we have women on board, we're done for. Cavallini sees all and tells all."

It was probably three in the morning and a little before the first light of dawn. But the clouds weltering over the Lombard shore obscured the sky, which meant that it would still be dark for at least another couple of hours.

Once we entered the port, the girls finally lay down to sleep in the couchettes. The two of us couldn't stretch out in the cockpit—it was still full of water—or unfurl the sails, so we walked back and forth along the lake under the lamplight, one eye on the boat and another on the windows at the Vittoria to see whether Cavallini would appear.

Above us the sky was clearing, but dawn was slow to arrive. It would be another two hours or more before the lake became visible through the mist. At the moment, the water was moved only by the sort of restlessness that follows a storm.

We climbed into the boat and without waking the girls, loosened the ropes and left harbor, pushing against the walls with our hands, so still was the air.

With a turn of the wheel and the aid of an oar, we disappeared behind the gardens of a villa within half an hour. Almost imperceptibly, the boat began to glide along the thread of a current along the coastline. We passed by Rèsega di Barbè, then the Villa d'Azeglio. The Cannero Castles could be seen standing out against the shore as if suspended in air, and the lake was so colorless it was hard to tell it from the sky.

"Let's go put up inside there," I said. "We'll have to rest today after the night we've spent."

We came ashore at the Gardanina in front of the castles, and from the women in the *osteria* I got the keys for the main one. The sun had meanwhile made a hole in the clouds, and a bit of air was beginning to circulate. One of the two girls, Wilma, put her head through the hatch. Behind her appeared the other, Milena.

"Where are we?" she asked.

"In paradise," Orimbelli replied.

They'd never been to the castles, and when we turned and they saw these abandoned fortifications emerging against the light from the glossy black water, they thought they'd crossed, while sleeping, not a lake but Lethe and Euonoë.

Accompanied by Dantesque quotations and the often obscene mythological allusions of which Orimbelli was a master, we passed the arm of the lake that divides the castles from the coast and went to anchor under the main fortification.

During our visit to the ruins, Orimbelli was with Wilma almost constantly, and she showed interest in his classical culture. I contented myself with the other one, Milena. She was the less attractive and more stupid of the two, and I almost regretted having picked them up; they seemed so simpering after our first few chats. I'd met them a couple of months before in a pastry shop in Laveno, and they'd looked as if they were classy, so much so that I was surprised to find them willing to go off for three or four days in the boat. I asked Milena what they'd told their families.

"That we were going a friend's in Milan," she said, "to

study together for a Latin exam. Instead of taking the train, we stayed in the station bar until it was time to set sail."

We rejoined Wilma and Orimbelli in the only habitable room of the fortress, a small round room carved out of the eastern tower, with the remains of some ornamental frescos. There, I regaled them with stories of the crimes of the fifteenth-century Mazzardi pirates, who'd come home after raids loaded with people from Marengo, and always with three or four women captured from the lakeside villages. They'd use them until they were finished with them, and then toss them in the lake like rubbish. One by one, they were washed away by the current, toward Cannobio, where they slowly sank to the bottom.

Unmoved by the fate of their predecessors between these walls four hundred years ago, Wilma and Milena behaved like honest prey. So I decided to keep them with us for all of the promised four days, and take them to Stresa and Baveno, too.

At the Hotel Suisse in Baveno we took two double rooms. One afternoon while I was taking a nap in my room, Orimbelli disappeared with Milena. He told the porter they were going to visit the Isola Pescatori. When I came down, I found Wilma sitting on the terrace holding a book she'd brought along in her bag.

I had a gut feeling, so I went up to the room where Orimbelli was staying with Wilma and put my eye to the door. I heard his voice, then Milena's, saying he was horny.

Not again, I thought as I went back downstairs. But I said nothing to Wilma and took a walk around the town looking for the Villa Fedora, where I'd seen the musician Umberto Giordano.

I found it, but the gate was closed. A man came out from behind the villa with an armchair over his shoulders; he stopped when he saw me. He must have been a thief, stripping the residents little by little. I asked him who lived in the villa.

"No one," he replied. And off he went with his armchair.

I returned to the hotel to find Orimbelli sitting in the garden with Wilma and Milena.

"We just got back from Isola Pescatori," he said.

VII

—

THE NEXT DAY we went back to Laveno, but the girls begged me to put them ashore at Cerro; they'd walk home from there. I complied, and we got off at Cerro, too, to go with them as far as the village. While Milena and Wilma went to the station to scan the schedule so they could say when they got home that they'd just got off the train, we went to have supper in a trattoria.

We made our way slowly back to Cerro in the dark to sleep in the boat. I was walking beside Orimbelli, who was silent and absorbed, when all at once, it occurred to me to tell him something that had been on my mind since the day before.

"Orimbelli, you don't stand on ceremony, do you? A couple of days ago at Stresa: Charlotte. Yesterday at Baveno: Milena . . . You regularly dine from my plate."

He didn't deny it. "Put it down to weakness," he said. "I should respect others' women, but I can't. But also, it's my view that women don't belong to people. It's not as if they can become the property of this fellow or that. They're free to choose, or to make sure they're chosen. All the same, if I've taken advantage, you'll have to excuse me. But in the first case as well as the second, I didn't have the impression I was stealing anything or betraying anyone. It was a case of *res nullius*, no one's property. Or rather, something abandoned, left for others' discretion. In legal terms, a scrap, leftovers. I helped myself to your leftovers; that's the best description of my behavior."

There was nothing I could say to that.

"And yet," I said to him, "*your* leftovers—I haven't yet had the chance to see how they taste. You never throw me a thing. What I mean is, you never add anything to the mix. Could it be that you don't know any women to invite onto the boat?"

He was very embarrassed and started making a mental list of everyone he knew.

"Well, I don't have a great stable here. Of course if we were in Naples, we'd need Noah's Ark, not the *Tinca*. But I don't know anyone around here."

"You don't know anyone in Intra?"

"Yes, I know a few people in Intra. I can try . . . In fact, we'll probably get her on board. She's a fine woman! Not really from Intra, but from around there: a pharmacist's wife. A woman of quality. Let's go to Intra and see what I can arrange with her."

We stayed at the port in Intra for a couple of days while Orimbelli came and went, phoning, sometimes disappearing for hours, bustling about finalizing this business with the pharmacist's wife.

To judge by his reports whenever he joined me on the boat or at the Leon d'Oro, it was no simple matter. The lady, who had two children, was waiting for her sister in Melzo to phone her to give her a bogus excuse to get away.

After two days' delay, she was finally ready to leave. She would go to Laveno on the eleven o'clock shuttle boat, and instead of taking the train, she'd slip onto our boat.

I hoisted the sails right away so we'd arrive in time to catch our prey. Orimbelli was extremely excited. It was a real sacrifice for him, because Armida was a highly emotional woman, and very proper. But to break even with me, he was going to have to arrange to leave us alone in circumstances that would make her surrender inevitable.

We were at the port of Laveno by ten. Seated on the dock with his binoculars, Orimbella kept the Intra jetty under observation. When the shuttle boat set off, he climbed back into the sailing boat.

"It's done. She must be on her way by now."

He moved toward the arrivals area and got into position to watch the passengers disembark.

The shuttle boat docked and just as instructed, Armida got off with her suitcase and purse and went into the waiting room for the Northern Line, as if she were going to take the train. But she let it depart without her.

Having inspected the square and the area surrounding the port, Orimbelli gave her a prearranged signal and she moved toward the dock. She looked about for the *Tinca* with a frightened expression, spotted it and descended the stairs that took her to the pontoon where it was docked. Orimbelli emerged at the appropriate moment, took her case and offered his arm to help conduct our prey into the boat.

Thanks to careful surveillance the operation was secure, and Orimbelli quickly stepped off the jetty and jumped aboard. The lady was already safely below deck. We then raised anchor and set sail for Luino as if there were nothing going on.

She'd come aboard so quickly I hadn't had the chance to take in anything apart from the fact that Armida was gigantic. The *Tinca* complained, too. As soon as it felt her weight, it dipped on one side as if blasted by a sudden wind. Once we'd moved away from the shore, the signora struggled through the doorway and appeared before me in all her glory: a large woman of about forty, with a double chin, saggy breasts, wrestler's arms and a small, turned-up nose between fleshy cheeks, just like all fat ladies.

Orimbelli settled her on the bench and sat across from her to compensate, if only partially, for the boat's listing. A good wind carried us toward Luino.

When she heard where we were bound, Armida shrieked, "For heaven's sake! My husband has a brother in Luino and his house is right by the harbor!"

"So we'll go to Cannobio," I said.

"Cannobio? I lived there for three years before I got married. Everyone knows me there."

"We could turn back and head toward the lower end of the lake," Orimbelli suggested. "Solcio, Lesa or across from there, Arolo or Ranco."

At five that afternoon, the signora was feeling ill, so I dropped anchor at Sasso Moro, close to Arolo, near the mouth of a stream and under a canopy of branches that hid the boat completely.

Orimbelli had his own plans. He hurried to the village and came back again to say that he'd found a double bedroom. However, since it was risky to take the signora to the hotel, he would sleep in the village and leave us the two couchettes.

Despite his objections, I gave him the place in the boat, and after we ate, I went to the village to stay at the Albergo Milano.

In the morning, I headed back to the river at around eight and saw the boat practically submerged on one side. I realized that the two of them were in one couchette, and to avoid disturbing them, I took a walk through the fields and came back an hour later.

With the boat at anchor and the signora still feeling sick, there wasn't any point in setting off. Orimbelli kept wanting to leave me alone with Armida, but in the space of a few hours she'd turned into something of a clown, with her clothes and her face all mussed up.

"This is madness!" she said as soon as he'd gone. "What a circus! If my husband realizes I'm not at my sister's it'll be a disaster. I've two children and I'm pregnant with the third. But that man is so charming and romantic, I'd do anything for him."

"It takes half an hour in a taxi from here to Gavirate, and from there you can take the train to Milan. You'll be at your sister's in Melzo by the afternoon, and tomorrow you can return to your husband and children in Intra. You've spent a night now with Orimbell . . ."

She was offended. "I don't understand what you're trying to say. I spent a night with Orimbelli? Yes, but that man is a gentleman and I can assure you that he behaved himself. It was only this morning that he sat on the edge of my couchette. What dignified behavior! A real cavalry officer!"

When Orimbelli returned, the signora was ready to leave for Gavirate. He took her there after lunch and returned to Arolo in the same taxi.

"You'll forgive me," he said, climbing into the boat, "but as far as women go, as you said, she's all I've got—or nearly. However, you have no idea what you're missing. Armida has her special ways—unique. A pregnant woman . . ." And he lost himself in descriptions of the unbelievable curves on that giantess, her creamy skin and other exquisite bits that correspond to various cuts of veal: haunch, loin, rump, shoulder, rack.

"Do me a favor," I interrupted him. "You got Signora Armida at the fun fair, not the pharmacy."

He didn't open his mouth again until that evening, when, all tucked up in his couchette, he felt he had to wish me good night.

VIII

———

WE'D BEEN SKIMMING THE LAKE with variable luck for almost two months, and our last cruise had kept us away from Villa Cleofe for over a week.

"It's time to go home," said Orimbelli. "If we don't, they'll take us there by force."

His words conjured up such a wonderful image of Villa Cleofe—with Matilde, its fine food and the bishop's bedroom—that I turned the prow toward Oggebbio without even taking note of the winds.

When we arrived in the drawing room after climbing up an internal stairway from the dock, we found the women sitting quietly on the sofa just as I'd seen them for the first time.

I noticed that Matilde had left off playing the widow and wearing half-mourning. Perhaps now that her husband had officially been gone for ten years, she'd decided to change her life—or at least her appearance.

Signora Cleofe didn't ask what we'd been doing for the six days we were away, but throughout dinner Orimbelli talked about Ascona, Stresa, the islands and the beauty of sailing up and down the lake, day and night.

"One at the prow and one at the stern," he said. "Alone, in silence, blown about by gusts of wind, one passes one harbor after another. It's as if turning the pages of an illustrated book: constantly changing pictures and colors..."

He came to the description of the nocturnal storm that had surprised us, as well as the girls from Laveno. He didn't mention them, but he bragged about his sang-froid.

"In the midst of the gale," he said, "the facade of the villa appeared between flashes of lightning. Just a bit more, and we'd have crashed into the wall. It was maybe about three, and I saw a light go on in the bishop's bedroom."

"That's right," Signora Cleofe acknowledged. "On the night of the storm I took a turn around the rooms to make sure all the windows were closed."

Orimbelli went on. "Storms apart—and in any case they're rare—the spectacle of the lake is something indescribable. You can't imagine what the shores look like from the middle of the lake. All the different villas, the inlets and streams, the waterfalls in the mountains, little villages..."

"Why don't you try it yourself?" I said, turning toward Matilde. "Just for half an hour, in front of the villa. Then, if you get a taste for it..."

Signora Cleofe looked at me with an air of pity, expecting a negative reply from her sister-in-law. But Matilde immediately said that she'd come with us the next day for a little turn in front of the villa.

•

She came aboard the next afternoon dressed in white piqué and with a blue scarf over her hair. She gave me her arm and climbed into the boat. When she lost her balance, she leaned, sighing, against my side. That was enough for me to understand just what she was made of, inside and out. I realized she cherished this accidental contact—the first reward, perhaps, of the new life she'd decided to embark upon.

When the boat caught the wind and began to list, she was momentarily alarmed. But after half an hour, nothing could frighten her, not even the waves that now and again splashed over the side and divided round the gunwale. She sat below the bridge, enraptured, her hands gripping the bench. With her face to the wind and her bust erect, she resembled one of those eighteenth-century figureheads with rosewood breasts splitting the billows under the bowsprit.

Orimbelli was manning the jib at the prow. Every now and then he looked at his sister-in-law, worried lest she feel sick what with the pitching, rolling and gybing caused by the wind, which had now risen to gale force. It wasn't the usual inverna but a devilish tramontana, the kind that clears the lake of all craft and threatens even the lifeboats.

"We'll have to hug the coast so we won't rock so much. Let's go back to the villa," I said.

"What a shame!" Matilde exclaimed. "I'm having a world of fun."

To keep her happy, I had to stay in the middle of the lake until evening. The boat ran back and forth like a greyhound.

•

At table Matilde asked me with the greatest seriousness if I'd be prepared to recruit her as part of my crew.

"Of course," I replied. "I'll have a full crew then, and I'll be able to introduce myself to the Stresa Yacht Club as master of my own boat. It was with that club, an old sailing academy on our lake," I told her, "that we began yachting like true Englishmen in the Borromeo Gulf. At the end of the nineteenth century it was Ceriana the lawyer, the Marquis Dal Pozzo and Prince Troubetskoy. Count Lele Borromeo, the nobleman Tirelli, Giovanola di Cannobio and the others came later."

Matilde was excited by these names. "Let's go now!" she said, looking at me earnestly.

I reminded her that she'd have to get hold of the right clothing—sundresses, shorts, espadrilles, bathing suits, a few sailors' hats and a waterproof jacket, since there could be rain and bad weather.

"I have everything already! So I'll be ready tomorrow at eight," she replied.

Signora Cleofe couldn't believe her ears. "Have you lost your mind?" she said.

"No," her sister-in-law replied. "I just want to have a life again. I'm thirty years old, the war is over, and I'm not a widow anymore. What should I do? Wait to grow old in this house?"

Signora Cleofe shook her head and said nothing further.

The sun wasn't up yet, but a red glow behind Luino forecast a clear, windy morning, the kind that comes at summer's end. Like a woman changing her clothes, the lake sheds its subtle, light colors after Assumption Day in order to put on an intense sky blue, sometimes a deep turquoise if the tramontana sweeps across it in the morning and the inverna again in the evening.

I opened the balcony window and looked at the lake, which passed before me like a river in full flow. It was as smooth as oil near the shore—protected as it was by the Cannero promontory and the one at Carmine before that. But two or three hundred meters out, as far as the eye could see, the waves bounded ahead, beyond Santa Caterina, Arolo and Ranco. There, it usually becomes calm again, exhausted by the great race.

I'd woken up while it was still dark, excited by the wind and the thought that in the morning, Matilde would be coming with us on a three- or four-day expedition. It was a sure thing that I'd get close enough to catch her scent, to see her in her swimsuit, touch her on some pretext, help her back onto the boat after a swim or out of it on jetties that were too high at some of the ports. One thought followed another, until I came to the problem of nights in the boat. Where would she sleep? Certainly not outside the cabin on the cockpit, where Orimbelli slept under canvas out of nostalgia for the tents in Africa. Below deck there were two couchettes with barely more than seventy centimeters between them and a four-inch keelson toward the prow, the mast at the foot. She'd sleep in one of the couchettes, and Orimbelli and I would sleep side by side outside under the canvas. But when we lay down, partly undressed, she'd see that we were uncomfortable, and it would be silly to leave one couchette empty...Who was to say that she might not invite me to sleep below deck? She certainly couldn't invite her brother-in-law; in this case, a stranger would be less out of place than an in-law. I'd be able to hear her breathing in the dawn silence, more anxious than the night's. My arm, having fallen out of the couchette, might meet hers while we were slumbering. And hand in hand, we'd both pretend to sleep, until a quiver under her skin would tell me I could go up her forearm, to her shoulder—she'd be calm and quiet the whole time—until I reached one of her breasts. Just one of them—like a fairy's chalice, or the Holy Grail—would be enough to give me a foretaste of that sublime nectar, or one of those miracles only love can bring about. I'd relish it, a little at a time, day and night, with Orimbelli there, but blind.

These were a boy's fantasies, and they always came to me under some pretext in the hours before dawn. But the sun would flush them out and scatter them, since a breast is a breast—a bit of flesh and skin. Just like a foot is a foot, and nothing more.

I was sitting on the bishop's bed with the electric light on, not sure if I should lie down again, and looking around for something to read so I wouldn't slip back into the excitement of those fantasies, when I heard a faint noise—a mouse gnawing at the corner of the door? I looked over and saw the knob turning silently, as if someone were trying it from outside.

It's her, I said to myself. And all at once I understood Matilde's passion for the sailboat. Her protracted isolation had taken its toll: at the first appearance of a man, she'd lost all reserve, and after a dead calm of ten years her blood was roiling like a lake during a storm.

I looked around. I always slept without pajamas, in a vest that stopped at my navel. I grabbed my trousers, stepped into them and went to the door. Someone had started up again, scratching the wood next to the lock.

I'd got into the habit of locking the door when I went to bed. Cursing this useless precaution, I began turning the key slowly so as not to make any noise. Slowly, slowly I opened the door and waited. First a slipper came forward, then a leg.

Alas! It was Orimbelli. I looked him in the face as he glided into the room, suddenly realizing that I didn't know him at all. I wondered what thoughts and plans were hidden behind his high, Mongolian cheekbones, his deeply furrowed forehead.

"Excuse me," he whispered, "but I haven't slept all night. From upstairs I heard you open up the balcony, so I came down to talk to you. It's about something urgent and extremely important. I've been anxious since yesterday. I would have come just after midnight, but I thought the women might hear me. Right now they're sound asleep and we have time for at least a couple of hours' talk before we set out on our journey."

Curious to hear what he was about to tell me, I had him sit in the armchair next to the bed where I was lying down.

He rested an arm on the bed and began. "When I came back here from Naples, I hardly remembered that my wife had Matilde in the house. I met her in thirty-three, when she was scarcely more than a teenager, at the time she got engaged to my brother-in-law. She was a skinny thing, and plain, but rich, an orphan from a very well-off family: the Scrosati. That was why my brother-in-law wanted to marry her. In thirty-six, I went to Africa voluntarily, but my brother-in-law, an engineer, was sent there against his will and put to work in the Genio regiment making roads and bridges for the war. He left here without having had time to post the banns, and he counted on coming back soon. Instead . . . may I count on your discretion as a man of honor? On your silence regarding what I'm about to say? You see, it's a serious matter. Delicate."

"Of course you can!"

"Good." He continued. "It's not true that my brother-in-law fell in a counterattack during the Battle of Ascianghi Lake. He was captured by an Ethiopian unit formed by the natives of Hollegga while he was finishing a road for armored cars with his colleagues. They were all killed apart from him, and he was taken away with them. Unfortunately, they cut off his . . . you understand. Which means, he's no longer a man. And yet his life was saved."

"So then—he's alive! And he might come back one day or another," I said.

"No, he's not coming back. Apart from anything else, he doesn't have the courage to turn up in front of Matilde or any other woman without his thingies. And besides, he's also become Ras Naghèta's right-hand man. He's doing well and has stacks of money. He even managed to escape from prison in India during this war. Now he's an Ethiopian citizen—with a passport, no less. I found out last year from an Abyssinian diplomat in Rome."

"But why haven't you said as much to Matilde?"

"I talked to him in forty-one, before I left Ethiopia for Naples. He told me everything and said that since he was a *spadone*, he wanted to stay in Africa for the rest of his life."

"What's a *spadone*?"

"Someone without thingamies, but not without . . . you know. So although he's not able to have kids, he can probably still have women. Some castrati have this facility, but most of them are out of the game. Anyway, he decided to disappear from his pre-Africa world. If he's a *spadone* of those who . . . all the better for him: he won't hurt for 'madams'—that's what they call women of color down there who get together with whites. Before he left, he made me swear not to tell anyone what had happened to him. 'Lost' or 'dead' was fine, he said, didn't matter. 'As long as they think I am no more.' "

"But when you found out, couldn't you have spoken to your sister-in-law when you came back home last year? She was still waiting for him."

"I swore. And besides, what would the point have been? The ten years have already passed, the marriage was invalid, and my wife was already talking about declaring her brother 'presumed dead.' Anyway, Matilde never loved him. The family wanted the wedding in order to marry off an orphan and also to join two considerable estates. Love never came into it. Love came afterward, for her and for me. Yes, my friend, that's what I came to tell you. I love Matilde and I'm loved by her in return. It's a tragedy, believe me, a real misfortune!"

He bowed his head over the bed, almost at my feet, as if he wanted to cry.

"It's both my tragedy and my good luck," he began again, raising his head. "My despair and my hope. Because at this point I'm living only for that woman. I'm crazy about her. Yesterday evening I had the impression that you were looking at her in a certain way . . . Maybe you were thinking that by recruiting her as your crew and taking her around, something would end up happening . . . and as far as women go, you've got credit with me. I can't blame you if that's what you were thinking; you couldn't have imagined the truth. But Matilde is just waiting for a chance to be alone with me—like a prisoner awaits liberation. Because she loves me, and because it's the first time in her life. That's why she pretended to be into sailing. Yesterday in the boat, she was trembling with fear, and she said she'd never enjoyed herself so much. She finally saw some light, some happiness! For a year, we've only been able to speak to each other two or three times. We touch each other's feet under the table, our arms brush against each other, and once we even managed a kiss on the stairs. But my wife never lets us out of her sight for a moment. She doesn't trust us; she's suspicious!"

I was nonplussed, and had to acknowledge that if this was how it was, the two of them were perfect dissemblers. I was also a little disappointed, because it would have been worth a whole season of silly young things to be able to snare Matilde. What a devil! I should have expected a trick like this from Orimbelli.

"I'm confiding in you as I would in a brother, or a friend," he began again, "and because it's better to say certain things at the outset, before there can be misunderstandings. I realize that everyone has the right to seduce a woman. Women belong to everyone. But I wanted to tell you that we have feelings for each other. It's an overwhelming passion, and I don't mind telling you I'd risk my life for it."

"You've done the right thing to talk about it," I told him, "and not to mince words. I'll be sure to respect your feelings."

He rose. "I didn't doubt it. You're a fine gentleman! A true friend!" He shook my hand warmly and tiptoed out, closing the door gently behind him.

Daylight began creeping through the brocade drapery at the window. Soon the sun would flood the bishop's bedroom, rendering it violet rather than red in the first light, and transforming it into a first-class mortuary with its canopy, the altar-like chest of drawers, the walnut wardrobe with large panels, the prayer stool and crucifix between two purple festoons.

I stretched out on the bed, staring ahead to the wall where the door had opened and Orimbelli had gone out of the room. Reflections rose up from the lake, just lit by the sun, in the form of luminous circles, moving up the wall to the ceiling, dissolving and changing shape like jellyfish. I traced those fleeting forms, so like the words Orimbelli had just uttered. A game of light: elusive, vague and improbable, yet nevertheless present, and perhaps a sign of other circles that would form and dissipate during the remainder of the summer.

IX

___

THE *TINCA* DEPARTED QUIETLY with its new cargo, but without an appearance from Signora Cleofe, even though it was already ten o'clock. Matilde had a genuine sailor's bag and a big suitcase, as if she were going away from home for two weeks.

As soon as we left the dock, I thought we'd head toward Cannero. I wanted to hurry away from the area around the villa and the gaze of its *padrona*, who was surely watching us from behind the shutters at one of the windows.

Heading north, I found myself in front of the villa of Pasha Emanuele Zervudaki, a mysterious character who'd come to the lake from Turkey about twenty years before. Some said he was the son of a cook from Cannobio who'd gone into the Sultan's service, while others took him for a real pasha with a harem. Still others thought he was a Greek from Salonica who'd made his fortune in the Balkan wars.

Zervudaki was a tiny man somewhat resembling his contemporary, Vittorio Emanuele di Savoia, who shared one of his names. He was permanently irritated, as short people always are. I wished he'd show up on the balcony or in the garden as he had before, so I could insult him in return for his once having told me off for mooring at one of his buoys.

I looked at the tall palazzo overlooking the lake and thought of the Sublime Porte, the seraglio, the eunuchs and, by association, the engineer Berlusconi. As I understood it, he lived in a small Abyssinian court at Lechemti, served and revered, but castrated —while his wife was starting to claim the natural rights denied her for so many years by the law and social mores.

I found the wind too strong, so I turned into it, and in less than an hour we could see the gulf of Intra. But the strong tramontana was waiting for me in the central basin, having circled the Zeda mountains. I decided to turn my back on the islands; treacherous gusts would surely be swirling around them. Cutting across the lake at its widest point, I went to shelter in the small, sandy bay of Polidora behind Cerro point, a place to escape the storms at the center of the lake. I'd been shown it ten years before by Togn Fisinessi di Cerro, a great shipbuilder. His father, also a shipbuilder, had made the *Cozia* in 1890, and Prince Troubetskoy was still sailing it in '35.

At Polidora, I left the two of them in the boat as agreed with Orimbelli. I said I had to see to a business matter in Laveno, but would return before evening. Instead, however, after walking to Laveno, I took the train inland and traveled around for a couple of days. I spent one day at home and then I went to pick up Jolanda, called Landina, a young woman I'd met on my return from Switzerland. I harbored some feelings for her, but I'd left her in her village so I could play the field during the summer—one of the last, I thought, before I'd have to turn over a new leaf.

I didn't feel like being the third wheel with Orimbelli, or standing in for the emasculated Berlusconi, who lived in Ras Naghèta's palaces and huts, lost to the world. Besides, I'd promised Landina the month of September, the best one for sailing, and we were now at the end of August.

I returned to Polidora with Landina when Orimbelli and Matilde had already spent two nights there. It was afternoon, and the *Tinca* looked abandoned. It was floating at anchor and roped to a plant as I'd left it, but with no sign of life on board. I called out. No response. There was nothing for me to do but strip down and enter the water in order to get to the boat and climb aboard. But while I was taking off my shoes, Orimbelli emerged from the hatch on the prow.

"We were sleeping," he said. And he scowled at Landina.

Once introductions were made, Matilde immediately attached herself to my friend. I'd told Landina the story of my boating companions during our train journey.

When I was finally able to look comfortably at Matilde, I didn't see the least sign of satisfaction or disappointment on her face. She seemed like any wife the day after the wedding: composed after an exhausting night, and wearing the mystery of encounters or clashes no one, apart from the protagonists, ever knows the truth about. I wished I could understand how things had gone, what kind of blaze there'd been after such a long wait—or if there wasn't one, as can happen, what a bitter disillusionment it had been instead.

But her face remained impassive, perhaps even studiedly so in order to show her indifference, her coolness. Orimbelli, on the other hand, seemed like a nesting blackbird. He was fully attentive to Matilde and treated her like an invalid—or someone he'd offended and from whom he now sought pardon for an abuse of power. It was his way of flaunting his achievement; things had surely gone well. But Matilde was trying to play it all down. She was irritated by her brother-in-law's attentions, spurning them when he overdid it, as if to demonstrate that they didn't amount to anything memorable or out of the ordinary.

Polidora is close to Ceresolo, a hamlet abandoned last century after a plague and now inhabited only along the road that cuts across the end of the promontory. The church, blocked up since the plague, was perhaps full of skeletons. It faced the lake and the small grassy square in front of it; the only shadow cast across it is that of the campanile, now silent. The houses near the church, long since abandoned, are empty, their plaster crumbling. A quiet spot, and for the next two days it became our parlor. We lay on the grass or sat like Turks, chatting and sipping cups of tea. For hours, I taught Orimbelli how to tie sailors' knots with odds and ends of rope, while the two women exchanged confidences. At night, we slept in the boat, Matilde and Landina in the couchettes, us two on the bridge. We had to let the strong tramontana blow itself out, which usually takes three days.

On the third day, when the winds resumed their normal patterns, we hoisted the sails to go toward the top of the lake.

As soon as she began to feel hot, Landina went below deck and reappeared in a black two-piece swimsuit. She was thin but nicely shaped. Orimbelli didn't fail to give her the once-over, but he suddenly panicked when he saw Matilde sitting on the bench completely clothed, with only her forearms bare.

"Why don't you put on your swimsuit, too?" Landina asked her.

Matilde blushed but didn't move.

Orimbelli, at the helm, was terribly embarrassed. He wanted to show off the riches in his possession, especially to me, but all the same, it irritated him to allow me even a glance.

"She doesn't have one with her," he said.

"No, no!" Matilde retorted. "I brought two with me."

Orimbelli exploded. "Then get undressed and enjoy the sun!"

Matilde went below deck and a short time later reappeared in a slightly outdated yellow swimsuit. It covered her up almost completely, leaving only her legs and arms exposed, but revealing the beauty of her body, which was of a milky whiteness, firm and round as an egg. When I saw her from behind, bending over to pick something up, I understood what in a woman is called "the power of the hips." In that area of her back which narrowed like the middle of a cello, I detected the strength of a whale's tail. She had little room for maneuver, but in that small space she could have wiped out Orimbelli and the entire Somalian troop of Aimone Cat to which he'd belonged.

That afternoon, while we docked at the abandoned jetty in Maccagno, it was time for everyone to go swimming. Matilde swam slowly, gliding through the water without making a splash. When she returned to the boat and stretched out on deck beside me to dry off, Landina and Orimbelli were still out in the lake, busy swimming a large expanse of water. Matilde's thin jersey suit stuck to her wet body like a second skin. Now transparent, it revealed a dark triangle as wide as a hand and two chocolate-colored aureolas surrounding her nipples, whose points had turned as rigid as the tip of an umbrella in the cold water.

I tried not to look at her, or at least not to show myself too curious, so as not to embarrass her. But I couldn't take my eyes off her body, which seemed to have have me locked in a fight to the death.

When Orimbelli climbed back into the boat and saw the effect of the wet swimsuit on his sister-in-law, he couldn't restrain himself. "If you have two suits, go and change! Don't you see what you're revealing?"

Matilde looked at herself, then went into the cabin. She took two linen handkerchiefs and slipped them under the suit where her breasts were; the two points and the aureolas that had so alarmed Orimbelli disappeared. She returned to the deck and lay down in the sun.

That evening while I was preparing the boat for the night in the nearby port, I found myself alone with her for an hour. Orimbelli had gone to the old Osteria della Gabella to order supper, and after he left, Landina decided to have her hair cut at one of the village salons.

There was a long silence, during which each of us looked around for something to do. Matilde, with her back to me, was pretending to lace the cover to the mainsail. "I'd like to know what you think of me."

"I think you're dangerous because you're beautiful, but also because of your intelligence and your future."

"But what do you mean!" She was astounded. "You can see into my future?"

I explained. "I mean the future development of all the possibilities I can see in you."

"Please explain a bit better."

"I meant that during ten years of passivity, and with a temperament like yours, a late developer's, you've built up an alarming strength. I think I've seen the first sign of it in the way you've grasped your freedom. Anything is possible for you now. Orimbelli has only been the spark that lit the fire."

"Maybe," she admitted with an ambiguous smile. "But go on. Continue with my horoscope."

"I'm saying that you needed someone to awaken you, to reveal you to yourself. But now that you've scented the wind, you'll make your own way, by yourself. Which road you'll take, I can't say. But I'm talking about a life that's full in body and in spirit, one that a woman like you can endeavor to enjoy." I was grasping for words just to get her talking, and far from having a specific point. But I felt a need to calm my apprehension.

She remained thoughtful. Then, still not looking at me, she said, "Maybe you're right. But I've begun badly. I've been unlucky. And you are partly to blame."

I showed my surprise, but she wouldn't let me talk. She went on. "Yes! When I grabbed your flying invitation to come with you on the boat, when I pretended to be enthusiastic about the idea of going around the lake, how could you have failed to understand? Why did you go off as soon as we arrived at Polidora, and leave me in my brother-in-law's hands? Had you arranged it beforehand? Is that how you sell a woman?"

She turned to look at me and repeated: "Is that how?"

"I haven't sold anything," I replied. "I knew there was an understanding between you."

"What understanding!"

"Wasn't there? He told me himself, in my room, the night before you came aboard."

"There was no understanding between us and there has never been anything between him and me. But when you left us alone to go and pick up your girlfriend, I realized I'd been cruelly tricked and that I had to submit to it. I felt like a slave whose master has brought her home from the market."

And that makes three, I said to myself. I had to acknowledge that Orimbelli had always been more adept at taking my prey off me. Beginning with Charlotte and then with

Milena, he'd managed to snatch the tastiest morsel right out from under my nose. The one it was worth running around after for an entire summer—or the whole of one's life.

Having let it all out, Matilde went back to her pointless threading of the rings on the sail cover, and I realized, watching her, that she must be the one I'd got stuck on without knowing it. From the time I'd started searching, as a boy, for the other part of myself, the part that continually eluded me, I'd followed it in vain during my early youth, then in the breaks during the war and my periods of internment in Switzerland.

She was the one. But I hadn't been able to spot the anxiety on her face, or the near-desperate look she'd thrown my way when I'd uttered that fatal phrase at table only a few days before: *Why don't you try it yourself?*

I hadn't understood, and I hadn't dared to understand, just as all the other times. And that's how, by being too considerate, I lost the best in life. Orimbelli had understood everything right away. He'd muscled in and made the hit like a pro. Like Aimone Cat, he was all about timing. In fact, he'd say, whenever he talked about the war in Africa, his colonel and former general had had the ability to intuit the enemy's moves and to preempt them, sometimes with a forced march, sometimes with an immediate retreat.

Meanwhile, since we hadn't arrived at the restaurant, Orimbelli must have become suspicious. Although we hadn't noticed, he'd appeared on the pier above us in time to hear the word "market."

I looked up and saw him.

"What market are you talking about?" he asked with a fake smile.

"Matilde was asking me about the Luino market, where we're going tomorrow. It's a big market, a sort of fair," I replied.

"And Landina?" Orimbelli realized she wasn't there.

Matilde suddenly turned round. "She went to sort out her hair, but she'll be back soon."

And in fact Landina arrived ten minutes later. We all went to supper at the Gabella under a pergola of cherry laurels, between the lake and a game of bowls.

The next day we actually did go to the Luino market. We wandered around stalls selling chiefly camouflage cloth, uniforms and assorted provisions from the American army, which had recently liberated Italy from the Germans.

From Luino we went to the Cannero Castles, then to the Borromean Islands, passing offshore of Villa Cleofe.

I kept hoping for a chance to continue the conversation with Matilde that Orimbelli had interrupted. But I didn't manage to exchange a single word with her. In the rare moments when she found herself alone with me, she looked for some reason or excuse to curtail my attempts.

X

WHEN IT SEEMED ADVISABLE to return to the villa, Orimbelli begged me to let Landina out at some nearby port. If his wife should see us as couples, two and two, she'd understand everything, he said.

Landina waited for us at a hotel in Luino while we turned up again at Oggebbio: the three of us, just as we'd left it.

Signora Cleofe didn't even try to detain Matilde, who for her part thought only of getting away again. But just before supper, while her husband was still in his room and Matilde was helping Lenin to set the table in the dining room, she came into the drawing room where I was absorbed in my own thoughts, and said quietly to me, "I know what's going on and I hope your intentions are serious. When you've finished your little tour of the lake, I trust your hearts will lead you in the right direction." She went into the dining room, leaving me no time to respond.

I was lost for words. Signora Cleofe was convinced that I was getting along well with Matilde and could just decide to marry her. I wondered how long I could play along with this hoax. I decided to say a final good-bye to the Villa Cleofe and its inhabitants by the end of September. Perhaps, I told myself, I'd do well to put an end to this story right away. All I'd need to do would be invent some excuse, set sail for Luino tomorrow morning—alone—and never show up again.

I was sitting on my own in the drawing room with these new thoughts when Matilde came to tell me that dinner was ready. Wearing a dark, old dress, she looked just as she had the first time I'd seen her. She came over to my chair, put a hand on my shoulder and said with a sad smile, "Shall we go to the table?"

I got up right away and found myself face-to-face with her. She looked into my eyes, smiling bitterly. I decided to take advantage of the moment to test the situation. I stretched out my hand and caressed her face. Her lids began to close and she bent her head toward my hand, squeezing it between her cheek and her shoulder.

The gesture was enough to allow me a bit of hope. I'd have to play this game to the end; I'd started it, and it could reveal the path I'd always looked for. It might not lead to the marriage Signora Cleofe wanted, but take me down another, less straightforward and more difficult route. Such an undertaking would involve a clash with Orimbelli and result in altering the fate of more lives, above all mine, if it happened at a breaking point, as I thought it would. I knew by intuition rather than experience that in every game of hearts, there's hidden drama; it's set up and fed by the frivolous diversions and carefree intoxication of love. But it was no longer a game for me. It was a testing ground, a battle from which I expected to emerge as injured as I had to be in order to become a man at last, and to end an adolescence not even the war had managed to cast off.

That night in the bishop's bedroom, I tossed for hours in the snare I felt myself caught in, with the result that I became only more entangled. I saw Matilde's soft flesh yielding under the hands of Orimbelli at one hotel or another during warm nights on the lake: *my* flesh, which I'd unconsciously "sold" to a stranger, to that glutton, separating it, through a sorry error, from the love that was meant for me.

The next morning, the 21st of September, we left for a week's cruise. Around eight, Domenico and Lenin started helping Orimbelli load his bags onto the *Tinca*. Matilde was still in her room.

Just like real captains who board only when everything is ready for departure, I sat in the dining room with coffee and milk, butter and jam, waiting for Martina to bring me just-fried eggs and bacon from the kitchen for breakfast. She normally rose late, but Signora Cleofe was already stirring around the house. She saw me in the dining room and came to sit at table with an unusually kind demeanor. I realized that she wanted to speak to me, and she opened the conversation right away.

"I had a few words with Matilde yesterday evening," she said, "but she's rather impenetrable. I don't wish to speak to Mario. May I know from you how things lie? I'm not curious; I'm worried. I want to calm down. Tell me: Do you have genuine intentions . . . "

"What can I say?" I replied. "I was thinking about it only last night, and seriously. But you'll understand that some things—"

"Enough, enough," she said. "I don't need to hear more. If that's how it is, only a question of time or discretion, very well. As long as the intention is there."

During the conversation the signora sat with one hand over the other on the table, trying to look into my eyes. She got up and went into the drawing room.

Half an hour later she was on the balcony waving us off as we set sail for Luino.

Landina was waiting on the dock, having seen us from the window of the Albergo Ancora when we were halfway across the lake. She got into the boat and was happy to hear that we'd be wandering around for a week, going from one port to another.

She knew it would be the last bit of freedom for her. In fact, the past few days had brought her a letter from the States announcing the imminent return of her husband from prison. She'd told me in great confidence the day before, asking me not to let Orimbelli or Matilde know a thing about it.

"If, after five years, I can manage to find some purpose in life with my husband, all the better. If not, I'll stay on my own at my mother's."

Landina's father had died in the First World War, and she'd married at twenty-three, in '40. Six months later her husband was called back to the army. In May of '43 he'd

been captured by the Americans on the Brombaglia penin-
sula, east of Tunisia. He was taken as a prisoner to America,
first to California and then to Hawaii, where he had to stay
until the summer of '46. But he was now in a hospital or san-
itorium in Norfolk with pulmonary complications, and was
expected to be discharged after Christmas. In January he'd
embark on a Liberty ship direct to Livorno or Naples.

Orimbelli suggested that we take advantage of the tramontana to get to the Borromean Islands. We actually arrived just
after midday, in time to lunch on the terrace of the Albergo
Delfino just above the jetty at Isola Bella.

That afternoon we went from Isola Bella to Isola Pescatori,
and toward evening we dropped anchor in the port of Pallanza,
once more at Orimbelli's suggestion. I guessed that my friend
wanted to sleep with his Matilde in a good bed on land, and
in fact he suggested it as we docked. I proposed the Hotel
Beau Rivage, and said I'd sleep in the harbor with Landina;
I was afraid we'd be cleaned out by thieves during the night.
He was sure I was right, and he got off with Matilde and their
bags, promising to come back later for supper with us at the
Ristorante Milano, where we could keep an eye on the boat.

During supper, Orimbelli seemed brooding and preoccupied. When it was over, Landina and I walked the two
of them to the lobby of the Beau Rivage, where I saw each
of them take a key from the porter. Orimbelli hadn't dared
ask for a double room, though he surely expected to get into
Matilde's during the course of the night.

Landina and I stayed up late, sitting and chatting outside the Caffè Bolongaro. She'd been having second thoughts, even regrets, ever since she'd had news of her husband's certain return.

She looked toward the lights of Stresa. "I waited for him for so long," she said. "But last year when I met you, I sometimes couldn't remember his face or even his voice. We lived together for such a short time. In one of his letters to me, he wrote that often he couldn't summon up my appearance. It must happen to everyone during a long separation. But now that he's returning, I remember him so well! I feel as if I can already see him, even if I discover that he's changed, and find it hard to recognize him. In his last letter he says it's time we have a baby. And to think he'd only have had to wait another six months and he'd have found me just as he left me . . . But I don't regret a thing."

"You're right not to feel bad about it. Maybe Penelope did the same thing, not with one of the men who wanted to marry her but with someone we don't know about, someone anonymous, who'd be sure to disappear when her husband returned or she decided to remarry. We can't wait for anyone; no one is waiting for us. Each of us lives and loves however, wherever and whenever he can."

This was empty talk. An attempt, for her as well as for me, to adjust to living in the world. Not so much the one that was emerging after the war, but the world as it always is—bitter and difficult for everyone, all the time.

Toward midnight, she went to the boat. "I'll join you

right away," I said. "I'll have a smoke and then come down, too."

I wasn't sleepy. I walked a little way to the mausoleum of General Cadorna and then returned to the port, walking below the plants, and headed for the boat. By chance, I glanced at the road and saw a yellow light from the lamp of a bicycle slashing ahead of it. It was one of those bikes we rode at the time, with the dynamo screwed on to the front fork and a little wheel inside the tire.

I drew back into the shadow of a magnolia. The bicycle came closer and slowed when it got to the little slope near the Ristorante Milano. By the light of the streetlamps, I thought I recognized the man pedalling as Orimbelli. Perhaps he was coming to the boat. But he passed by the harbor without turning, climbed the slope and set off in the direction of Intra.

Was it really him? And if so, where could he be going at this hour, already after midnight? Where had he found the bicycle?

I went to lie down on my couchette without saying anything to Landina. But I couldn't fall asleep. I asked myself who the devil Orimbelli really was. At his house the day before, when I went to the bishop's bedroom for the night, I'd found him hurriedly closing the chest—just like a thief— with his initials on it: T.M.O.

"Temistocle Mario Orimbelli." I repeated it to myself, almost as if those three cabbalistic initials would serve as the key to unlocking the mystery of his life—if there really was a mystery to it, and not merely the tactlessness one sees in all good-for-nothings, which serves to furnish them with the choice cuts at all times and in all circumstances.

A month before, during a stopover at the Cannero Castles, he'd confided in me that his wife was sure he had a lover in Intra. And it couldn't be the pharmacist's wife, but someone else much younger. Probably the one he'd brought from Naples, as Cavallini implied.

Maybe he was on his way to see her on a bicycle lent him by the doorman, after spending a couple of hours with Matilde. He was certainly capable of that and more. That was supposing he actually was the cyclist I'd seen go by, and it wasn't someone who vaguely resembled him.

XI

—

I WAS WOKEN BY THE BELL of Pallanza parish church sounding the hour for Mass. It was Sunday, in fact, and I'd slept till nine.

As soon as I popped my head out of the canvas, I saw Matilde and Orimbelli on the pier, their bags at their feet.

"I realized you were still sleeping and didn't want to wake you," he said.

With the bells pealing through the air, we left port and headed for Santa Caterina. I'd hardly slept and I felt tired. It promised to be a splendid day, and as the shore receded, we could see the little island of San Giovanni near land, with Castagnola point just beyond. Clusters of leaves, already red or yellow, showed up against the dense foliage. Autumn was creeping around the lake that year like an unseen servant, silent and stealthy, but quick in his movements, as if it were his duty to change the backdrop scenery for the last act of a play.

During the crossing, I told Matilde the story of Beato Alberto Besozzi, who had become a hermit several centuries earlier on the sheer cliff in front of us, after surviving a shipwreck in the same waters we were sailing.

"Before the shipwreck, the Blessed Alberto was a merchant, or rather, a moneylender who did business in the villages around the lake. One day, his small boat capsized when a storm overcame him. He managed to swim to shore, just at the foot of the rocky wall.

"He was from Intra; he'd made money there, spent it, found women, had friends and enemies. He went back home, where perhaps he had a wife and children. But the shipwreck had opened his eyes. Enough, he must have said, I've no wish to struggle further. I'll stay here and eat *alborelle* carp and salad. And in fact he never left the grotto in which he took refuge. The fishermen brought him fish, the peasants dropped vegetables over the cliff for him and no one disturbed him.

"From time to time," I concluded, "I think about becoming a hermit myself . . . retiring in some remote place away from all these struggles. And more than anything, from the world's disappointments."

I wanted her to understand through indirect reference that I'd suffered a blow, and that my disillusionment was strong enough to make me want to spurn life.

In the small church, which rested on a limestone incline, Orimbelli, Matilde and I had to feel our way to the altar, it was so dark inside the sanctuary. I went over to turn on the switch and immediately a crystal coffin beneath the altar was illuminated. The body of the saint appeared, lying on a cushion of white silk, his hands and face browned and crisped by the centuries. He had on a golden cope, and his miter was askew.

I switched off the lights and the coffin, which was shaped like Orimbelli's trunk, was dark again.

It's possible to spend an entire day in the Sanctuary of Santa Caterina, wandering through the various passageways, arcades and cloisters, all of them infused with the atmosphere of other eras. Under an arcade of ogival arches, Orimbelli found a fresco showing skeletons in a country dance.

"I don't like this place," he said. And he hurried toward the *osteria*, with its four rooms and a small veranda hovering over the water on stilts.

We sat down in the early morning shade to look at the lake. The islands rose up from afar. Up closer, on the other shore, the cube that was the Albergo Eden showed up white against the green of Pallanza Point. The other milky cube—the Regina Palace and the Grand Hotel of the Borromean Islands of Stresa—looked like huge cetaceans stranded on the shore. Below us, the *Tinca* strained at its mooring, light as a cork.

The owner of the *osteria* came to tell us that she'd make us a risotto with bass for lunch. Orimbelli was easily persuaded to stay, but he wouldn't take a brief walk with us while we waited for the risotto. He didn't move from his spot beside the balustrade where he leaned back on the chair, staring into the distance, his arm resting on the gray stone surface. While the women started to walk up the hill, I asked him what he was looking at.

He replied without turning around. "The summit of Zeda. I'm making triangulations. Because the earth, like life, can be measured in triangles."

I proceeded to join the women, but at the third flight of steps on the mule path leading to the edge of the cliff, only Matilde sat on a low wall.

"Where's Landina?" I asked.

She pointed toward the summit, and with a sweeping gesture invited me to sit down beside her. She lowered her head and in a harsh, toneless voice said of my friend, "What a shame for that woman! She's so sweet and likable."

"Why?" I asked.

"Because I thought you were free."

"I am—free."

We sat very close to each other on the wall. Matilde looked at the ground without replying. After a long silence, she raised her head and looked at me with those eyes of hers, always frightened. A strand of hair had fallen across her forehead. I gently put it back and placed my open hand over her temple: it was burning. I wanted to draw her head toward me, but first I glanced above and below us.

Orimbelli was climbing up from the flight below.

I got up and began gathering blackberries from the bushes in front of me.

Orimbelli appeared at the turn. "The risotto is ready," he said sullenly. A moment later Landina arrived, and we climbed down together.

During lunch Matilde put her soft, fleshy calf beside mine under the table, while her brother-in-law ate in silence, his head bowed.

I had the sensation of being caught in a whirlpool—

or in one of those triangulations Orimbelli had been talking about.

As we sailed toward the top of the lake, Matilde asked me to let her take the helm while Orimbelli rested below deck. She sat beside me in her swimsuit, holding the tiller, and Landina, stretched out on the prow, kept a foot on the spinnaker so the jib would stay tight. Matilde came up close to me, brushing her breast against my arm and pressing against my right leg with one of her round knees. Eventually I put Landina at the helm and I went below deck to rest beside Orimbelli. Tanned as he was, stretched out with his hands crossed over his stomach and his eyes fixed on the deck's supporting beams, he resembled the mummy of Beato Alberto in every detail.

Our pace slackened and the hours went by with the quiet sloshing of the waves against the keel of the *Tinca*, allowing me to nap for almost two hours.

When we turned around the point of Villa Lavazza, the Gulf of Luino came into view. The inverna began to drop.

I went out and gazed at the sky, which looked menacing toward the west. "We'll spend the night in Luino," I said.

In Luino I decided to sleep in the hotel myself, but not in Landina's room, since she had stayed there the night before and the owner recognized her.

At eight we sat down to eat, but Orimbelli's mood was so remarkably dark that not one of us made the slightest attempt to initiate a conversation. I tried suggesting that we stay at the Albergo Ancora the next day, in case the bad weather should continue, but no one responded.

Our supper was about to end in silence when a marshal from the *carabinieri* entered the hotel. He approached the desk and spoke to the owner's wife. She pointed to our table.

"Is that your boat, the *Tinca*, anchored in the port?" he asked.

"It's mine," I replied.

"Then who is Signor Orimbelli?"

Orimbelli blanched. "It's me," he said, his voice barely audible.

"Your wife was found dead this morning at Oggebbio. I received a message at noon from the station at Intra."

"My wife?"

"Signora Cleofe Berlusconi Orimbelli," the marshal confirmed.

"But how did she die?" Orimbelli asked.

"The message did not say," the marshal replied.

Only then did I notice that Matilde had silently collapsed in her chair. Landina was spraying her with water from the table; she seemed to have fainted.

"Is it possible to find a taxi?" I asked.

"There are two outside the Varisene station," the marshal said.

I ran to get a taxi and returned to the hotel. Orimbelli, Matilde and Landina got in.

The journey around the lake, through Valcuvia, Besozzo, Angera, Sesto Calende, Arona, Stresa, Pallanza and Intra took more than two hours in the rain that had begun to fall. Orimbelli never once opened his mouth.

Domenico was at the gate of Villa Cleofe with a carabiniere, who accompanied us inside. In the drawing room we found the marshal, who took us to the first floor.

The signora lay heavily on her bed between two candles, as calm as if she were sleeping, and only a little bloated. Lenin and Martina were at her side. She was wearing a dark dress, her hair was combed, and her bare feet were tied together at the toes with a silk scarf. The dead woman seemed a cryptic response to our triangulations. The tranquillity of the lakeside villages, the peace of the azalea- and camellia-covered villas, our own excursions— all this was nothing but a beautiful shroud, concealing death. One had only to draw a curtain, open a wardrobe, switch on the lights in the dark to see the clues, the signals, the stop and go of the real journey.

"How did it happen?" I asked Lenin.

"Domenico found her in the dock this morning, drowned in her nightdress."

Orimbelli stood beside me looking at his wife. The marshal put a hand on his shoulder and asked him to follow him. The questioning had begun that afternoon in the dining room below. Orimbelli was grilled for almost an hour before it was Matilde's turn, then mine, then Landina's. We didn't have much to say, particularly because no one knew how to respond to the one question they asked concerning a precise fact. They wanted to find out if we'd known about a letter addressed to poor Signora Cleofe and found on her bedside table.

After midnight the carabinieri went off. Orimbelli, who'd stayed awake by drinking one coffee after another, joined us in the dining room, where the questioning had taken place.

"Suicide," he said. "Unfortunately. But I didn't see it coming. How could I!"

And he told us that as we were leaving the day before, he'd gone to the gate just before we set off and put through the mailbox a note addressed to his wife, asking for a separation. He'd decided to leave the villa with Matilde, who was naturally in agreement, in order to live freely with her until he could marry her. Evidently Signora Cleofe had not been able to withstand the blow and had thrown herself in the water overnight.

The marshal had found the letter on the nightstand in the signora's bedroom. It was handwritten on a piece of paper printed with the initials T.M.O. in red.

Matilde was shocked. "Why didn't you tell me?" she asked her brother-in-law. "I'd never have agreed to something like that. A letter? Writing a letter? Wouldn't it have been better to speak to her openly? And why such haste? Didn't we agree that we might not say anything this winter? And who told you I'd go along with it? That I wanted to live with you?"

Orimbelli didn't reply. He gave the impression of someone admitting to a mistake, but you could see that he wasn't actually displeased with his haste. He considered it unavoidable, fate, "already implicit in the matter," as he said before going to his room to sleep.

XII

—

OVER THE FOLLOWING DAYS, the public prosecutor conducted further in-depth investigations, taking up where the carabinieri had left off. It turned out that Domenico had noticed the letter in the box only that afternoon; that the signora, alerted by the gardener, had gone straightaway to fetch it, and that after reading it she had told Lenin and Martina to go ahead and return home to the lodge as she would not be dining that evening.

Already in the reports were declarations which indicated that at ten the following morning, when Lenin noticed that the signora was not yet up, she had knocked at the door to her room; that when there was no response, she'd decided to go in but had found the bed empty and not made up; and that she'd then joined Domenico and Martina in the search for the signora before she was found at the bottom of the dock.

The magistrate, having "verified," as he later wrote in his summing up, that the "two lovebirds" had stayed at the Hotel Beau Rivage in Pallanza on the night the signora drowned in the dock, ordered painstaking investigations into whether the chief suspect—as Orimbelli had unfortunately become—had not perhaps disappeared from the hotel during the night. Evidently not. The porter and the nightwatchman had noticed neither entry nor exit between eleven at night and eight in the morning. Matilde stated that Orimbelli had been in her room from eleven until half midnight. In the morning, he'd knocked on her door at around eight and stayed in her room waiting while she washed and dressed so they could go down to breakfast together.

All motorboat owners and drivers from Pallenza were asked whether they'd taken someone to Oggebbio that night. The answer to this, too, was negative.

Domenico, questioned by the magistrate, added to his first deposition. After we had left, he'd closed the iron gate of the cellar, which led to the dock. He'd hung the key as usual on a nail in the wall. It was becoming clear that in order to enter the villa, the killer would have had to be in possession of the entrance key or the key to the dock. He could have done without the one to the gate and climbed over the fence, but in that case, he couldn't have got inside without leaving some trace of a break-in.

Lenin said that when she'd come in with her key that morning, she found the ground floor windows and shutters firmly closed on the inside.

There were three keys to the entrance: Lenin had one and the other two were still hanging in the kitchen, where the carabinieri found them. It was evident to the investigators that at approximately 5 p.m. on the afternoon of September

21st—that is, after noting the contents of the letter Domenico had seen in the mailbox—Signora Cleofe had left the villa and gone to the village. Cavallini, in fact, had seen her near a mailbox at around 5 p.m. He couldn't say if she'd posted anything, but it was highly likely, since Signora Cleofe rarely went out, only once or twice a year, and then only in order to post letters personally.

The matter was put to Domenico, Lenin and Martina. The signora could not have gone out and come back in without being seen by one of them. But not one of them stated that they'd seen her—which seemed strange, although Domenico said he'd been in the greenhouse for almost an hour around 5 p.m. For her part, Lena said that at the time she'd been in the laundry in the cellar, washing clothes with the help of her daughter, Martina. The signora, therefore, could have put her head around the gatehouse and pushed the button to open the gate, which she then left ajar so it would be open ten minutes later when she returned from the village. It was an acceptable explanation. Less explicable was Lena's late statement, which emerged only in the second or third witness examination. She remembered noticing, when she entered Signora Cleofe's room on the morning of September 21st, that besides the unmade bed, there was an overturned chair. Both the marshal during the initial investigation, and the magistrate during the one following, had considered the theory that the body had been dragged from the room to the dock. Yet painstaking reconstructions had done nothing to confirm such a journey, which would have rendered credible the idea of a homicide made to look like suicide. But the upturned chair had to mean something. It could mean that someone had entered the room that night without turning on the light and had tripped over it, since it was usually near the bed. Or perhaps there had been a scuffle in the room, even a minor one. If it had been homicide, it was also possible to consider that the chair had been kicked over by the killer not on entering the room but on leaving it, with the victim thrown over his back in a dead faint or some other state of being unable to offer any resistance. But neither could one exclude the possibility that the poor signora had overturned the chair when she left the room, already intent on suicide. And that was the simplest and most plausible explanation.

Lena had repeated from the first interrogation that upon entering the signora's room at ten in the morning, she'd found the central light on, but not the lamp on the nightstand. This fact had given rise to new theories, but served to clarify nothing. The central light could in fact be switched on from the bed, using the cord. And it was logical that someone intending to go out of the room would use that in preference to the lamp on the nightstand, which Signora Cleofe normally used only for reading in bed.

After careful examination, the only theory that seemed plausible was that of suicide. Signora Cleofe, in a state of shock after reading and absorbing her husband's letter, had made her fatal decision: she'd gone down to the cellar in the night, taken the key to the dock off the hook, opened the iron door and thrown herself in the water. The door had in fact been found open, with the key in the lock on the inside.

It was possible to formulate one other hypothesis: if the alleged killer had had a key to the dock, it would have been simple—after entering the grounds—to go down to the shore, get into the dock from the lake, wade waist-high in the water, open the iron door and gain access to the villa's premises through the cellar.

There were two keys to the dock: one, which Domenico had used to lock up, and another that we kept in the boat, in a box underneath the wheelhouse.

The key theory wasn't neglected by the diligent magistrate. During my interrogation, he asked me whether I'd noticed the key missing from the box it was usually kept in, either temporarily or permanently. The question prompted me to remember the key, which should still have been in the box on the boat. The boat had remained at port in Luino, and the magistrate sent me there to get the key. It was in its place, among the tangled lines.

If it had only occurred to me to look in the box after passing the man on the bicycle that night in Pallanza! If I hadn't found it there, I'd have been certain that Orimbelli was the culprit and the next day, the reason for his nocturnal journey would have been perfectly clear to me.

But it hadn't occurred to me, and it would have been improper now to introduce into my deposition the hazy picture of the Pallanza shoreline that obsessed me: a man pedals toward Intra on a bicycle, its headlamp slicing through the night. It would have been unfair to identify, with hindsight, something that was more shadow than man.

The result of the investigation, the report from the carabinieri and the interrogation of everyone in the house plus ten other people, permitted the magistrate to archive the file under the heading: DOCUMENTS RELATING TO THE DEATH BY SUICIDE OF CLEOFE ORIMBELLI, NÉE BERLUSCONI. The postmortem examination had concluded "death by drowning" and ruled out any sign of violence on the body of Signora Cleofe; but it didn't fail to observe that she could have been stunned by a blow to the head inflicted by a heavy, blunt object—a bag of sand, for example—and then taken to the dock and thrown in the water.

Unfortunately, the suicide theory was never corraborated by a letter, not even a few lines written by Signora Cleofe. Those who voluntarily forsake their lives usually leave a message, a farewell, a phrase that serves as some explanation for their decision.

But proof of homicide, which in this case would have been more than premeditated, was lacking. So to the public prosecutor, it seemed only sensible to archive the file.

Orimbelli and Matilde made me swear not to leave them alone in this situation. To tell the truth, I'd never thought of leaving. I was keen to follow the investigation, because I hoped everything would be cleared up and Orimbelli would be seen to have had nothing to do with the death of his wife, even if the explanation was that he'd returned to the villa on the night in which Signora Cleofe had died, perhaps regretting having left the letter for her in the box and intending to get it back—or, if it was too late, to be frank with his wife about the reasons for his decision. I'd then have been free of any doubt. But none of it added up. As far as the investigation was concerned, suicide was the only possible explanation, and it seemed so self-evident that the law had to be satisfied with it.

Couldn't I, too, be content with it? I asked myself continually, reexamining, minute by minute, the time passed in the company of Orimbelli and the two women from the morning of the 21st of September until the evening of the 22nd.

In the muddle of the reconstruction and various theories, I came to believe that if Orimbelli had really killed his wife, he would have done it in order not to lose Matilde. He couldn't have been unaware that an understanding was developing between his lover and me. Maybe he'd been forced to consider the crime for fear that the love he'd temporarily managed to trick us out of would develop between us. In fact, now that his wife was dead, it would be possible for him to marry Matilde. Ah, the triangulation he'd spoken about while sitting on the parapet of Santa Caterina! He'd said it all: it was necessary to understand, and to act.

But whose turn was it to take action?

XIII

LIFE AT THE VILLA resumed its old rhythm. We always ate at the same hour, served by Lenin. Domenico worked in the garden and his daughter, Martina, stayed in the kitchen.

I slept as usual in the bishop's bedroom, Orimbelli in the little room on the top floor and Matilde in the room adjacent to that of poor Signora Cleofe, now closed.

At night, between sleeping and waking, I'd listen out to catch any sound or hushed voice that might alert me to Orimbelli's inevitable movements, but I never heard anything. Nights in my room were peaceful and silent, and the only thing I heard was the gnawing of woodworm in the wardrobe, where the red vestments of the dead Monsignor Alemanno Berlusconi had hung for twenty years.

The *Tinca*, which I'd fetched from the port of Luino, rocked in the dock in the spot where Signora Cleofe had been found. I'd tried a couple of times to say good-bye and go off in my boat. But Orimbelli and Matilde seemed so frightened by the idea of being alone in the villa that I'd ended up staying. Every now and again, I went to Intra or stayed in my boat, intent on some little job. I spent most of my time reading in a large study I'd discovered on the top floor, close to the little room Orimbelli occupied. Among all the books on physics and mathematics, which the frontispieces proclaimed had belonged to the engineer, Angelo Berlusconi, were some saints' lives that must have belonged to the bishop, and hundreds of old books that helped me to pass the hours of those long days between September and the end of October, while the inquest into Signora Cleofe's death was proceeding.

More than once after tea, which was always served under the copper beech between five and five-thirty, Orimbelli set down his empty cup and invited me to take a stroll through the grounds, as if he had something important to tell me. I always took the bait, sure that he wanted to confess his secret to me, and I followed him willingly to the end of the path behind the oleas. Below us, the shore had grown wider with the autumnal drought, and gentle waves broke soundlessly over the greenish stones of the lake bed. Surrounded by the scent of the *olea fragrans* and partially hidden among the leaves, Orimbelli would look around suspiciously before asking me:

"In your opinion, what would one need to spend in order to modernize this villa? I don't mean structurally, just functionally—perhaps the bathrooms, the boiler, the kitchen . . ."

I always answered him with random figures, aware that his question was a ruse and his aim to determine whether my voice or behavior revealed any change of opinion toward him.

Other times he'd ask me, in the same sly manner, what I thought of the public prosecutor, but he'd preempt my response with phrases like "What a magistrate! What objectivity! And what finesse!"

"Old-fashioned magistrates," I'd reply. "Philosophers, rather than judges or investigators."

The time I gave him that answer, he launched in and went on talking for half an hour. "Definitely," he agreed. "Philosophers, anthropologists and sociologists should be magistrates, and not investigators! Just think: the criminologist Lombroso, the great Lombroso, whom I've always considered a master, discovered, when he studied the skull of the brigand Vilella, that in place of the occipital ridge the outlaw had a depression as one finds in gorillas or chimpanzees. That's biological fatalism for you! Man does good or ill according to how he's formed. Those with primitive characteristics also have animalistic responses. If I had an occipital depression, for example... But feel it! Feel just here: Is there a depression? No, right? There's a ridge. And what a ridge!"

When I'd touched the back of his head to satisfy him, he asked me if it might not establish a line of defense. If I didn't think, to put it bluntly, that he could be passed off as crazy, if necessary—or that he might not actually be crazy. But when he heard that the documents had been archived and the whole sad case could be considered closed, he became the most normal man in the world.

I renewed my efforts to leave, but it was impossible. Orimbelli seemed terrified at the idea of being left alone with Matilde.

"You must stay," he told me. "At least until we're married. What would people say, and the staff, too, if we stayed on our own in the villa? You can consider the bishop's bedroom your own."

One night a storm broke out, the last of the year, accompanied by thunder, lightning and blasts of wind. We seemed to be in the middle of one of those blitzes of a few years before.

Awakened by the racket, it occurred to me that the *Tinca* was only secured in the dock by two thin cords between small poles. They might have loosened and untied themselves, or slipped off during the past few days. It wouldn't be the first time bad weather had sucked at a boat poorly secured in the dock and then smashed it against the shore.

I put on my trousers, tiptoed out of the room and went down to the ground floor, finding the steps by the light that kept flashing through the skylight over the stairway.

The *Tinca* was rocking peacefully, caressed by the undertow. I made sure the cords were fast and went back upstairs.

When I got to the first floor, I passed by poor Signora Cleofe's bedroom and Matilde's on my way back to my own, which was on the other side at the end of the corridor. I'd come to the foot of the stair that led to the mansard when a flash of lightning, aimed directly at the villa, vividly illuminated the corridor and the first flight of stairs in front of me. I saw Orimbelli sitting on the top stair, his legs crossed like an Egyptian scribe's. His eyes met mine and shone for a moment like a scribe's glass eyes before everything went dark again.

My hand was already on the handle and I went into my room, shutting the door behind me. I lay down the bed and wondered if Orimbelli were on his way to or from Matilde's room. I looked at the clock: it was three. He slept little at night, at least to judge by his appearance in the morning; he never woke before ten. Of course he went to visit Matilde. Then perhaps he'd sit for hours on the top stair surveying the corridor, in order to see whether I'd sneak into the room of his slave.

More than once, I sought Matilde's feet under the table, but in vain. She seemed to have forgotten our former touching and brushing against each other. I wondered why she no longer considered it appropriate, and whether the idea that she was morally complicit in Signora Cleofe's suicide had returned her to the lifestyle of the previous ten years, or maybe convinced her to join forces with Orimbelli. It was no longer possible to speak to her or to take up the conversation where we'd left off. Surrounded morning and evening by the two servant women, she was preoccupied with the successful running of the house, and I could never find her alone or with nothing to do. Orimbelli moved continually between one room and the next, popping up around every corner like a restless shadow. We met up only at table and at teatime and spoke of trifling household matters—about Domenico, who was becoming increasingly deaf, plants, flowers and everything else that seemed to us completely devoid of any reference to what had happened or its consequences.

•

I seemed to have become co-owner of the villa, the heir of poor Signora Cleofe. It was understood that I could come and go as I pleased, order the servants around, choose wines I liked from the cellar and make use of the small harbor and the dock, where I'd decided to leave the boat for the whole of the winter season.

At the end of November, Orimbelli and Matilde let it be known that they'd be married in Milan in a few days. They'd got used to each other on the *Tinca*, and it seemed to have brought them together sufficiently to face married life. Matilde had not expected it so soon, but it must have seemed inevitable when the results of the inquest into Signora Cleofe's death became public.

The wedding was to be celebrated without guests or publicity beyond the banns in Oggebbio and Milan. But the news quickly spread, and it became known that the Puricelli cousins had condemned it. To be precise, they let even the most distant relatives know that they were "condemning it." Cavallini spread the news in Oggebbio.

On the morning of the wedding, the four of us left for Milan together in a taxi from Intra: the bride and groom sat in the back with Landina, and I sat in front with the driver, as was right and proper. But at Fondo Toce, or rather, before we'd gone very far, Landina began to feel carsick and asked if she could change places with me. I went behind to take her place beside the bride, and found myself in contact with Matilde, our thighs and shoulders touching; the car was rather small. Orimbelli seemed indifferent. By then, he'd got where he wanted to be and was no longer pointlessly jealous or afraid.

I tried to pick up some message other than heat from Matilde's body: the pulsing of a tendon, a muscular contraction, some barely perceptible friction from her leg. But there was nothing by the time we reached the entrance to the motorway beyond Sesto Calende. When we got as far as Gallarate, her entire body moved, but only to stretch, and she became still again immediately afterward.

The marriage was performed in a side chapel of the Basilica di Sant'Ambrogio, Orimbelli's natal parish, and witnessed by Landina and by me. The priest believed in neither conversation nor advice and confined himself to handing the groom a small red book after the ceremony, a sort of passport stating that Temistocle Mario Orimbelli and Matilde Clelia Scrosati were legally married from that day forward.

"For the hotels," the priest explained. In those days illegitimate couples weren't admitted to hotels, or were forced to take separate rooms.

As soon as we were out of the church, Orimbelli ordered the driver to take us to the cathedral square, where he asked him to park. He crossed the piazza with us and went down the alley next to the Albergo Diurno Cobianchi, as if he wanted to take us for a bath or some other service. But then he turned to the right, toward the entrance of a restaurant that was fairly renowned at the time—the Tantalo—where we ate the wedding lunch as if it were any other meal.

I came to believe that the name of this restaurant, where I'd eaten so many times before the war, had purposely appeared before me like a trick of fate. Had Orimbelli not inflicted on me, for months and months, a tantalizing agony?

On the return journey, the last leg of which was made in the dark, the problem of contact came up again. Matilde kept close to me, but under the pretext of necessity, and without indicating that she found the slightest difference between my leg or anyone else's.

Two days after the wedding, the couple left on a trip they wanted Landina and me to take with them. They went to a hotel in Sorrento, where they'd booked a room with a seaview toward Capri. Orimbelli must have felt at home in Sorrento and Capri since he'd lived in Naples for four or five years. He promised, if I went with them, to show me some interesting things: to take me to Pompeii, for example, where he had an archeologist friend who would show us everything that had been found in the Lupanar, the old brothels. But Landina couldn't get away, and I didn't want to go by myself.

When they came back, autumn's display was over. The trees in the lakeside gardens were bare, but the evergreens stood out cleaner and darker above the pale shades of the mimosas, already nearly in flower.

Informed by a telegram, I was at the villa when they returned. I decided to stay with them until after Christmas, which by then was just around the corner. Landina came to spend a few days, and she often stayed over with me, sharing the bishop's bed, a small double.

•

Winter on the lake is very mild, especially on the Piedmont side, which stays green throughout the year. But evening falls suddenly, and in those years, there wasn't much to do apart from shut oneself up in the house in front of a fire to read, talk, sip vintage spirits or simply watch the fire. Anyone who's passed even a single winter in a villa on the lake knows just how much peace and how much boredom can be distilled into a single day. The spectacle of the water, which turns from steel blue to the color of lead under the winter rains; the snow appearing on the mountains; sunrise and sunset during good weather; the boats' toing-and-fro-ing; the reliably windy days; the flowering of the chrysan-themums, mimosas, camellias and finally, azaleas—all these things signal the season's passing. From behind win-dows, and amid old furniture from the period when the villas were built, the few who remain living in them see the passing of time in a way that's impossible in the city, or in apartment houses.

That's how I spent the winter months that year, with Orimbelli and Matilde, and also in the melancholy company of a shadow we couldn't escape. Toward March, when the winds began, it seemed to take advantage of every gust to insinuate itself into its old domain.

"I heard it last night," Martina once whispered in my ear as she served me my *caffè e latte*. "It was sighing behind the dock. Poor signora! I can't believe she killed herself."

Other times it was Domenico. After looking around,

he'd sidle up to me in the park and tell me he'd seen her early that morning, behind the steamy glass of the greenhouse.

It seemed the only ones who didn't see or hear her were the married couple. Whenever they returned to the villa after a couple of days away, I found them increasingly weary of their union, one as disillusioned as the other. Orimbelli would often put his arm through mine and draw me deep into the grounds, behind the olea bushes, on the rotunda facing the lake.

"I've been loved too much," he told me one day. "I don't mean by my wife, poor thing—she hated me . . . Yet the hearts I've conquered! But now I'm wondering, my friend, where all this love has gone. Can it have vanished like a cloud? And the love I've given, has it dissipated as well? Because even in the most trivial situations, with Germaine or Wilma, or Signora Armida, I've always expressed a certain amount of love. For me, love is a fluid, a disbursement, an emanation issuing from my body. And yet there's not a trace of it left in me."

"When did you first notice yourself running dry?" I asked him.

"I'm not sure. In the last few days."

"Have you tried going back to the first presentiments of this feeling? To look for the reason behind such a change? There must have been an event—I don't know—an incident, a trauma, as the psychoanalysts . . ."

He interrupted. "I hope you're not implying . . ."

"For God's sake," I reassured him, "I'm miles from implying anything."

"Good," he wrapped up. "Let's not refer to that. We'll not refer to it, ever. What happened, happened. I've simply allowed myself to let down my hair with you for a moment because I have no one else to speak to. But you misunderstood me. For that reason, we won't speak of it further."

So saying, he turned back toward the villa. I followed him meekly, and when he began discussing the weather and telling me he already felt spring in the air, I agreed with him.

"Yes," he said, talking to himself, "spring's on its way back, but not love. Because love is a mirage, a trick that lures us to the entrance of a splendid garden and then melts away and disappears, leaving us in the dark."

XIV

—

IN APRIL, when the whole of the garden was ready to flower, an unexpected snowfall frosted the mountains right down to the shore. Such an April storm hadn't been seen for forty years. Centuries-old trees fell down under the weight of the snow in all the gardens. A few kilometers away, in the villa that had belonged to Massimo d'Azeglio, a cedar of Lebanon split in two, and a moustache on the marble bust of the marchese even broke off on account of the sudden freeze, or perhaps a fallen branch.

In the grounds of the Villa Cleofe the most illustrious victim was the huge magnolia that rose on the side facing the road: an enormous tree, towering over the roof by several meters and almost completely hiding the house from view. The top, weighted down by snow, was bent and the trunk had collapsed at the level of the roof. The magnolia had the appearance of a giant with its head resting on its chest. The entire upper part had toppled over where it had broken above the lower branches. The wreckage did not constitute any danger, but with every gust of wind it began to groan at the breaking point, which was splintered and dismembered.

Now and again throughout the day, more often in the silence of the night, one heard the plant's sorrow, a heartbroken lament that came when the wind blew from the lake or the mountains.

On one of those nights, a little after the final disastrous winter snow, I was sitting at the fireplace in the dining room with the two Orimbellis and Landina. We'd dined well, almost happily, and for once, the habitual sulkiness of the married couple seemed to have given way to a better mood. The Brighenti couple had been to supper. The husband was an accountant and director of a bank, at least one branch and, as a lieutenant in East Africa during the war, he'd been Orimbelli's army companion. At table, therefore, we'd had to listen to stories of war and colonial life, but it hadn't bothered us, since Brighenti wasn't a braggart and he told a good story.

"Do you remember that time we found a well after three days in the desert?" he asked his friend. "Everyone ran to drink, but Aimone Cat stood up in his stirrups and cried, 'Animals first, then the men!'"

Orimbelli tried to change the subject, but Brighenti continued. "This fine fellow," and he pointed at Orimbelli, "was the first to throw himself in the water. So Aimone Cat, up on his horse, thundered, 'Captain, from now on we'll consider you a camel!' "

The Brighentis left around eleven. They were going to stay in their own villa at Premeno, above Intra.

The silence that had fallen over us since the guests' departure an hour earlier seemed to make us gloomier than on any previous evening. Temporarily transported to his days of glory, Orimbelli suddenly found himself before the fire with his own thoughts. No one could think of a thing to say, and the pressure to initiate conversation made the women tongue-tied, too.

In the silence we began to hear the moaning of the split magnolia. Every five minutes it whined like a soul in pain. Immediately afterward, the shutters creaked as if someone had passed through the air.

"It's the wind," Matilde said. "But that branch should be cut. It kept me awake again last night."

It was just before midnight. While he was waiting for the moaning, which seemed late, Orimbelli grabbed a bottle of wine from the table behind him and was holding it against the light to see how much was left when someone knocked on the shutter at one of the windows.

Matilde jumped up. "Who's there?"

"It's me, Domenico."

Matilde went to open the door and Domenico presented himself in the dining room.

"There's someone at the gate. He won't say who he is. He wants to speak to Signora Cleofe. He saw there were lights on the ground floor and he asked to come in."

"I'm coming out to see," I said, and I followed Domenico through the grounds as far as the gate.

I saw a man on the other side of the bars and I asked him what he could possibly want at this hour. He took off his hat and showed me his face. I'd never seen him before.

"I am Berlusconi, the engineer," he offered the words slowly, in a quiet voice, "Signora Cleofe's brother. Let me in."

In the meantime Domenico had recognized him and he opened the side gate to the visitor waiting to come in. I walked beside him up to the entrance, then fell behind as he crossed into the dining room.

Orimbelli was still holding the bottle in his hand and sat in front of the fireplace, but facing the door.

Berlusconi remained at the threshold. He looked at the women, trying, perhaps, to determine which of the two was Matilde.

Orimbelli put down the bottle, got up quietly and offered the seat to his brother-in-law, who put his hat on the table, sat down and began watching the flames licking the chimney.

He was a handsome man in his forties with dark skin, and completely bald. Still watching the flames, he finally spoke.

"Where is my sister?" he asked in a tone so sharp as to seem hysterical.

No one answered. When I realized that Orimbelli preferred that I speak, I said, "Signora Cleofe died between the twenty-first and twenty-second of September of last year."

Berlusconi started, but didn't take his eyes from the fire. "The twenty-first of September," he said. "And what did she die of?"

"She drowned."

"But you—who are you?" he asked as if he'd only just noticed he was talking to a stranger.

"I'm a family friend. Of the Orimbellis," I answered, indicating man and wife.

Berlusconi slowly drew back from the fire, maintaining his distance from his brother-in-law. Resting one arm on the table, he began to look at Orimbelli and Matilde, one after the other, as if to read on their faces the rest of the story I'd begun to recount. Then he lowered his head once more and said, "I get it. Everything's clear. My sister dies and you two get married right away, joining the Berlusconi legacy to the Scrosati." He turned to face Orimbelli. "But you knew I was alive!"

"You told me not to say anything. You renounced everything. You didn't want to come back to Italy . . ." Orimbelli protested, almost under his breath.

"Yes. But something compelled me to come back. Something specific. I knew very well that Matilde was free, because proxy weddings are annulled if they're not consummated within six months. But your union explains so much."

He turned toward me. "Where did my sister drown?" he asked abruptly. "In the lake? Out in front here?"

"No. In the dock," Orimbelli said. "She drowned in the dock after we made our intentions known. Before I went, I left her a letter."

Berlusconi stood up and picked up his hat from the table. "I left my suitcase at the hotel in the village," he said, turning to me, "and I did the right thing, almost as if I'd known! I'm off. But we'll see each other again."

"I must tell you," Orimbelli added, "that in February of this year, the Tribunal declared you presumed dead after ten years . . . We did everything according to the books."

"Well done. That way, as my sister's only heir, you become the owner of my estate, of my house in Milan and of this villa. Great! Tomorrow we'll talk! Tomorrow!"

I got up to accompany him to the gate. As we passed through the grounds, we heard the heartrending cry of the split magnolia just over our heads.

Berlusconi stopped and listened. The lament came again, quieter this time. He looked up. Although he realized it was the sound of a broken branch, he said, "It sounded like a genie, sneering, as they do in Ethiopia. But genies? They're here, too, dear sir."

I was at the port in Oggebbio by nine. For the past few days, I'd taken advantage of the good weather to beach the *Tinca* and have her repainted. I was working alongside an old fisherman from the area, sanding under the keel, when Berlusconi came out of the Albergo Vittoria. He saw me and walked down to the shore.

"I'm getting the boat ready for the summer," I told him.

"I see that, but I'd like to have a few words with you, if you don't mind."

We went to sit in the sun on a wooden trestle a little way from the boat.

"Have you known my brother-in-law for long?" he began. He spoke loudly enough to be heard at the end of the road—by Cavallini, who'd come out of his place to snoop.

"Since last summer," I said quietly. "I actually met him right here, where I'd stopped one evening with my boat. We became friendly and traveled around the lake together for the whole summer. After a while, Matilde joined us and we made a trio, in fact, a quartet, since the woman you saw last night also joined us. From time to time, we came back here and between one trip and another, I was a guest at the villa. So I met Signora Cleofe. During the final trip last year, while we were eating in a hotel in Luino, the carabinieri alerted us to the death of your sister."

"How long had you been away?"

"Two days. The evening before we'd stayed in Pallanza. They stayed in the Hotel Beau Rivage and I was in the boat with my friend."

"Pallanza, if I'm not mistaken, is about fifteen kilometers from here."

"More or less. But you're quizzing me for nothing. Go to the prosecutor in Pallanza and you'll find out everything. They'll let you see the file with the carabinieri's reports and the witness testimonies."

"I'll go," he said. "I certainly will. I want to get to the bottom of the story of my sister's suicide. You don't know my brother-in-law!"

"I know him well as a sailing companion . . ."

"You don't know who my brother-in-law is! Martina—is she still in the house?"

"Yes. Why?"

"Martina was seduced by that monster when she was eighteen. He deposited a fine sum for her and gave her a passbook to keep her family quiet and avoid scandal. And he volunteered to go to Africa. Now do you understand the kind of man he is?"

I was speechless.

Berlusconi nodded good-bye to me and went back to the hotel. After a bit he came out with his suitcase and got into a taxi he'd had called. I found out later from Cavallini that he'd transferred to the Hotel Beau Rivage in Pallanza.

XV

—

WHEN the boat was properly caulked and revarnished, I took it back to the dock.

I slept and ate with the Orimbellis, who'd sworn me to stay with them, thinking that Berlusconi would return. But he didn't. He remained at the Beau Rivage in Pallanza. He left it in the morning and returned to it in the evening.

It wasn't difficult to work out that he was looking into the death of his sister. He'd been to the proscecutor to see the inquest report and had questioned all the taxi drivers and motorboats from Pallanza to Intra, in Baveno and in Stresa. He spoke to the doorman every day, but without getting anything out of him. The doorman stayed at his post until midnight, and the nightwatchman didn't remember having opened the door to anyone at the time, either after midnight or before eight in the morning.

Berlusconi tried to see if he could leave the hotel one night after midnight using one of the service doors which was on a spring and could be opened without a key only from the inside. He managed to go out unobserved. Half an hour later he rang the bell and the night doorman came down to open up for him. In the morning, having gone out early, he tried to reenter the hotel between eight and eight-thirty without being noticed. Taking advantage of the temporary absence of the doorman, he achieved his goal without a hitch.

But it didn't prove anything. Discouraged, he was about to leave Pallanza, where he'd been for almost a month without setting foot in Oggebbio, when he ran into some unexpected good luck. Hanging about the old town, he found himself passing a cobbled street where there was a little basement bicycle repair shop. On a sudden hunch, he went in and asked the mechanic if he would rent him a bicycle until the next day. He was asked for a deposit, which he gave, and then he said he'd stop by that evening to get the bike.

"Before eight," said the mechanic, "because that's when I close the workshop."

Berlusconi went back to get the bicycle at seven-thirty and leaned it against a plant along the lakefront in a poorly lit area, securing it with a lock.

At half past midnight, he left the hotel while the doorman was sleeping in his cubbyhole on the first floor. He went to pick up the bike and started off in the direction of Intra. He got to the environs of the Villa Cleofe in Oggebbio in under an hour. He hung about for a long time, walking back and forth in front of the villa without meeting another living soul. Then, hiding the bicycle around the corner of a house, he climbed the villa wall, crossed the grounds and lowered himself over the breakwater to get to the shore. When he came to the dock wall, he removed his shoes, socks and trousers and entered the water.

He had to plunge in up to his chest to get inside to where my boat was because the water level was high, as it is every spring.

Mission accomplished, he went back to the beach, dried himself off with a towel he'd brought along, put his clothes back on, and crossed the grounds once more to get the bicycle. He rode back to Pallanza slowly. At eight, he returned the bike to the mechanic, paid the hire fee and went to the hotel. He mingled with a group of Swiss tourists coming out to the islands, then slipped into the dining room without being seen by the doorman, and ordered breakfast.

At nine he returned to the mechanic and asked how many cycles he rented out.

"Only the one," the mechanic replied. "It's mine. The one I gave you."

"Do you often rent it out?"

"Never. The last time was last autumn . . . in fact to someone like you, who came to get it in the evening and brought it back in the morning."

"Would you be able to recognize that person?"

"I think so," answered the mechanic. "He was a short guy, rather stocky, with slanting eyes and a crew cut."

"What sort of accent did he have?"

"From Milan, I'd say."

No one at the villa had heard the outcome of Berlusconi's investigation. The news had filtered through only via information from Orimbelli's solicitor, because Berlusconi had hired a lawyer to start proceedings to reverse his status as "presumed dead." He probably intended to return to Africa once he reclaimed what was his, or at least to disappear from the lake.

Orimbelli was anxious to hear of his brother-in-law's departure. "Let him take everything that's his and get out of here, that ill-omened bird! So I never have to hear his squeaking falsetto again, for any reason!"

However, he did have to hear it again.

I'd put the *Tinca* back in the water awhile before and sometimes I'd go for a spin in front of the villa. But Orimbelli didn't want to go out anymore, and neither did Matilde. They stayed in their separate rooms all day long and met only at table, often with me, where they never failed to carp at each other.

One afternoon at around one, while we were having coffee, Domenico came in to say that Berlusconi was at the gate.

"I'm not at home to him!" Orimbelli bellowed. "He can see his lawyer. At this point everything's in the hands of the lawyers."

Matilde paid no attention to him and signed for Domenico to let Berlusconi in.

Perched on the corner of a dining room chair, Berlusconi began a speech, as if he were standing before a court. He told us the story of his investigations and revealed that he was on the verge of exposing his sister's killer. He pointed angrily at his brother-in-law. The bicycle mechanic who'd rented out the bike to him had described him with such precision that there could be no doubt regarding his identity.

"But there's more," he dug in.

I stopped him and begged him to let me speak.

He looked at me, enraged, but calmed down right away when he heard me say I'd seen Orimbelli on a bike the night Signora Cleofe had died.

It was time I spoke up, and I regretted not having done so earlier. There was no need for me to pity or defer to Orimbelli. He'd had me snared from that first evening at the port in Oggebbio when, like a cat ambushing its prey, he'd watched me arrive on the last breeze. He'd coolly studied me while I hauled down and as I moored and prepared the boat for the night with the meticulousness of a straightforward or even witless person. As soon as I was on land, he'd craftily questioned me in order to reel me in. He'd taken me first for a coffee and then to his house, perfectly sure that I wouldn't escape from his traps: the villa, his sister-in-law and of course, the bishop's bedroom. And that's how he recruited me to take him around so he could carry out his misdeeds. He'd involved me in his schemes and made use of me as a convenient witness for the defense, when I should have been the one to accuse him.

I was irritated not only by the risks I'd run and might still incur, but also because all at once, Orimbelli seemed the embodiment of all the waste and profligacy I'd abandoned myself to that year, indeed, a sign of the waywardness of my life, a deviation in its course which I would have to correct without delay.

"I wasn't sure it was him," I said, "which is why I kept quiet. I left him at the Hotel Beau Rivage as he was going up to the room with Matilde. It seemed unlikely that two hours later he'd be riding his bike along the lake at night. But after all you've discovered, I'm convinced it was him and I'll state it in front of anyone. I might add that one day in Ascona, he looked into the uses of aconite. It can be used to treat trigeminal neuralgia, but it can also send a close relative to another world."

"You're both crazy!" screamed Orimbelli. "The conclusions of the public prosecutor are worth more than your gossip. I didn't have the keys! How could I get into the house?"

"With the keys in the dock," Matilde said, her voice low and trembling, "which you'd have taken from the box on the boat and then replaced."

At these words, a precise memory took shape in my mind. After the death of Signora Cleofe, I'd gone with the marshal to Luino to retrieve the keys to the dock. When I took them from the box in the boat's stern, I noticed that they were no longer tied to the line I'd secured them to a month before, having worried that they might slip into the water and get lost while someone was handling them.

"You're right." I turned toward Matilde, who seemed, like me, to have shed an unbearable weight. "The key was untied from the cord and was definitely used that night by your husband. He'd have put it back in the box during our trip to Santa Caterina, but he didn't bother to reattach it for fear we'd notice his trick."

"But there's more!" Berlusconi cried out in his tiny voice. "Much, much more!"

Orimbelli could stand it no longer and attempted to fling himself at his wife. Berlusconi and I simultaneously got between them. At that, Orimbelli left the dining room, pounding on the door and crying: "Cowards! I'll kill all of you!"

"There's much more," shrieked Berlusconi, scrabbling in an internal pocket. "Look at this letter!"

Frantically, he took a couple of sheets from an envelope and offered them to me.

I took them and began to read.

"Read out loud," said Matilde.

I started from the beginning.

Oggebbio, 21 September 1946

Dear Angelo,

I've had no news of you for months, but I assume you're well as usual, and that your silence is due to your travels in the interior of Africa, where it seems you have business, as you wrote in one of your last letters.

I'm writing today to tell you something new and, for me, troubling. I feel the need to tell someone in my family, and you—no matter how far away or how lost to the world—are the only person I can turn to.

This afternoon, the gardener, Domenico, came to tell me that there was some correspondence in the mailbox next to the lodge.

I went to see, hoping it was a letter from you, but I found an envelope with no stamp on it. Inside was a brief missive written in Mario's hand, telling me that he was in love with Matilde, that she duly loved him in return and that they had therefore decided to leave the house in order to live together while they waited to formalize their union in some way. He'd put the letter in the box around eight in the morning, just before going for another trip on a large sailboat with Matilde and a friend he's made recently.

I'm very surprised by this letter, and I can't make sense of it. If he wanted to bring me up to date regarding his disgraceful liaison with Matilde, he should have done so when he was leaving the house for good, and not before a boat trip from which they'll return in a few days.

The letter I have in front of me makes me think, and seems a curious warning of something that's about to happen.

I wish you were here. But unfortunately you decided to disappear long ago, and our correspondence remains absolutely secret.

Out of respect for your instructions, I've put forward the request that you be declared "presumed dead." I thank you for the generous bequest from your part of the inheritance, but you should know that it will always be at your disposal should you decide to return.

I close this letter with great affection for you, and I will go to post it straightaway.

Yours,

Cleofe

The envelope remained on the table. I read its strange address: TO SIGNOR DR AMEDEO GUERRA, NR MOHAMET ALKACEM, ADDIS ABABA. Directions followed for the name of a street I couldn't decipher.

"It's the name and surname I took down there; they're on my Ethiopian passport," said Berlusconi.

He sat down, somewhat calmer, and reported that his sister had always known he was alive, although after '41 he hadn't been able to send her any news because of the war. At the end of '45 he'd begun to write to her again, and to receive her letters. He'd received three. The one I still had in my hand was the third and last; unfortunately, it had arrived six months late.

"Where has Mario gone?" Matilde suddenly asked.

"He won't have gone far," said Berlusconi. "But we must have him arrested immediately." And he invited us to follow him. He'd left a taxi in the village and hoped to go directly to the public prosecutor with the two of us.

At the Albergo Vittoria they told us that the cab driver

had realized that Berlusconi was going to make him wait a bit too long, so he'd gone to take a client to Cannobio, but would be back within half an hour. Berlusconi was put out but agreed to wait—under the eye of Cavallini, who never let us out of his sight and tried to guess what was going on.

More than half an hour had gone by and the taxi had still not returned when Domenico suddenly ran up. He went to Matilde and whispered something in her ear.

"Something's happened," she said. "We must return to the villa immediately. Mario seems to have done something crazy."

Berlusconi came along and Domenico accompanied us to the first floor.

The door to the bishop's bedroom was ajar, and Orimbelli appeared to be sitting on the floor with his back against the door, his head bent over his breast.

I went nearer and saw that his body was folded over at a right angle, and only his feet touched the floor; they reached close enough to brush against the chest bearing his initials, T.M.O. A thin but extremely strong cord dangled from the doorknob and circled his throat—the one I'd kept in the little box in the boat's stern along with the keys to the dock, and which he'd surely taken from my vessel.

XVI

—

"A HANGING A LÀ CONDÉ," the doctor explained. He'd come with the public prosecutor that evening for legal certification.

"Rare, but not unusual. The Prince of Condé—not the one Manzoni wrote about, who slept the night before the battle of Rocroy, but Louis, the last of the Condé—hanged himself from the handle of a window and gave his name to the technique. There are cases where people hang themselves from a headboard, raising themselves up a bit and slipping the head through the noose so that they drop suddenly into a sitting position. The weight of the body pulling on the noose is enough to cause the occlusion of the upper airways and compression of the jugular vein, with subsequent loss of consciousness. It's therefore impossibile to save oneself in case of a change of heart."

"Very interesting," Berlusconi remarked. "In any case, justice has been done."

While the doctor was speaking, the public prosecutor found a letter on the bed, folded in two, which no one had noticed. He unfolded it, read it and passed it to Matilde, who handed it to me after she'd read it. Berlusconi didn't even want to look at it. There were few lines:

Everyone is against me. No one loves me anymore. I don't have the strength to fight the accusations that will be leveled against me.

You will never know the truth. I have no remorse and I am perfectly calm. On my tomb I want this simple inscription:

TEMISTOCLE MARIO ORIMBELLI
1906–1947

The letter was unsigned and it spread across a sheet of paper printed with the same initials he'd used to write to his wife—T.M.O. It was impounded by the public prosecutor. After he'd arranged for the removal of the body and an autopsy, he sought Matilde's consent to carry out a search of the house in order to look through Orimbelli's personal effects for further confirmation of the statements made by Berlusconi and me.

He was shown the little room Orimbelli had slept in before and after his marriage, the marital bedroom and finally, the bishop's bedroom and the chest with the initials T.M.O.

Domenico had gone to fetch chisel, hammer and pliers, and with his help the chest was opened.

Under a captain's uniform there was a military sword, a dagger, a German machine pistol, a 9 mm revolver and a Winchester rifle, each wrapped in a piece of canvas. Below these, packets of letters tied with string and each bearing a name. I read some of them: Fanny, Lina, Bruna, Luciana,

Marisa. They were letters from women, all of them dating from his time in Naples. In a corner of the chest, inside a leather hatbox, there was a hard hat of English make; inside, on Morocco leather, it bore the intials T.M.O. in gold. Among other odds and ends—horseshoes, Maria Teresa dollars, pipes and ivory objects—there was a pocket compass, a black brassiere, two or three pairs of women's underwear, long silk stockings and velvet suspenders of every color.

"War souvenirs," said the public prosecutor.

Some legal tender banknotes to the value of one million lire were found concealed in a sort of large pocket in the lining of the lid. It was all he had.

When the officials had gone, the problem of whether I should stay or leave presented itself. Could I stay under the same roof, that night and the ones to follow, with only Matilde there?

It was she who solved the problem by calling on Lenin and her daughter to sleep in the late Signora Cleofe's room, which communicated with her own.

"I'd be grateful if you would not leave me alone, at least until the funeral," she said.

We ate together, seated across from each other. Both of us were surprised by the strange talkativeness that possessed us. As if to distance ourselves from the mental image of Orimbelli hanging from the doorknob, we spoke nonstop about nothing in particular, while Martina came and went from the kitchen.

I asked Matilde if she'd ever lived in Milan. She'd been waiting for nothing more than the chance to speak, and began to tell me about her life, starting with her childhood.

Her mother had died of typhus when she was ten, and two years later, her father also died of a heart attack. Her father's sisters were given custody of her, and at twelve she was sent to boarding school in Aigle, Switzerland. She spent the next six summers in the institute's holiday home in the Vallese mountains, only returning to Italy when she was eighteen. She had a secondary school diploma and intended to enroll at university to study medicine, but she had to take care of her aunts, and when they died in succession within a couple of years, she was left heir to their material goods.

Before she died, the last aunt arranged Matilde's marriage to Berlusconi, one of Milan's most eligible bachelors. It was only on condition of this marriage that Matilde's inheritance from her aunts would come to her. She was therefore persuaded to go through with it. Things, however, were hampered when her fiancé was suddenly called to arms. Nevertheless, her aunt made her marry by proxy, after which she wrote her will and died.

I knew the rest, more or less. Yet I remained curious about one thing, and I couldn't satisfy my curiosity while the maids continued coming and going from the kitchen and listening to our conversation, if only in snatches.

I let Matilde know that I wanted to ask her something without being heard by the maids, and she signalled for me to wait.

At last Lenin retired to her room. Martina stayed a little longer in order to make us a linden tea. "It will be good for you, signora. It'll make you sleep," she said as she served it.

"Thank you, Martina. You may go to bed now—I'll be coming up right away. Please leave the door open between the two rooms. I'm afraid to be alone!"

As soon as Martina had gone, I tiptoed around my question, playing with words and employing euphemisms. But it came down to my asking her whether Orimbelli was the first man she'd slept with.

Without the least sign of being upset, she answered, "No. I had an affair nobody knows about. I'll tell you about it briefly. During the war, between forty-one and forty-three, I worked for the Red Cross in a hospital in Milan. I was twenty-three, and Berlusconi had been dead for some time, as far as I knew. A doctor—married, with children, unfortunately—fell in love with me. He was a professor and head physician, and I admired and looked up to him. A truly charming man . . ."

"I understand everything," I said. "But Orimbelli? What did he say when he realized, at Polidora, that you . . ."

"He really tried interrogating me. He suspected it was Berlusconi during our engagement. But I cut him short, telling him it was my business."

I couldn't find anything to say and remained silent. I thought about the way a woman will admit previous relationships to a man she's just met and is already in love with. She'll always speak about smiles, bowing, hand-kissing or at most, light caresses—innocent role play, mere trial runs for what she'll do with the real lover she's finally discovered. But despite such caution and reserve—which is often her modesty and respect—how can one avoid thinking about how others have used her?

She continued talking, perhaps guessing where my thoughts were going and hoping to interrupt them. "Now that you know everything, even things a woman should never tell, may I ask you something?"

It was a question I hadn't expected: whether or not I intended to marry Landina. It was now down to me, my turn to be precise.

"I'm not going to marry Landina," I told her, "because she's already married. Her husband was captured by the Allies in Tunisia in 1943, and he returned from the States a few days ago after three years in prison. He's kept in contact with Landina and she's been waiting for him for a long time."

"Landina's married!" Matilde exclaimed. "But I never saw her wear her wedding ring!"

"She was ashamed to wear it."

Matilde drank her linden tea, now cold. "What a heat wave!" And she fanned herself with a handkerchief.

It was almost midnight and I knew she wanted to go to bed. Not to sleep, so much as to go over the events of the last twelve hours in peace, including the unexpected revelation of Landina's marital status, the last dramatic turn of this curious day.

I accompanied her as far as the door to her room, and then went down to the dock to sleep in one of the *Tinca*'s two couchettes, at least for that night. Climbing into the boat, I thought: one can't escape here: neither in the bishop's bedroom, where Orimbelli hanged himself, nor in the dock, where Signora Cleofe died.

The following evening I opted for the bishop's bedroom, which was at least comfortable.

Orimbelli's burial took place in Milan, not in the Berlusconi family tomb at Cimitero Monumentale nor in the Scrosatis', but in common ground at Musocco. Only Matilde and I were in the car behind the coffin. We left Oggebbio early, as when we'd gone sailing, and the taxi came to pick us up at Intra. It was the same one that had taken us to Milan a few months before for the wedding, with the same driver.

The ceremony was rushed through and took only a few minutes. Matilde spoke with the undertakers about what Orimbelli wanted on the headstone and how to position it, asking them to send her the bill at Oggebbio.

The funeral over, I thought it only right to ask Matilde to lunch in a restaurant on Viale Certosa. Also, I didn't want to say good-bye to her on the street, since I'd decided to stay in Milan for a day or two. The restaurant was close to the cemetery and groaning with the relatives of those who'd been buried that morning. It looked as if there wasn't any room for us, but a waiter managed to find us a little table, so narrow that as soon as we sat down, our knees met—reluctantly, I'd say, since this contact was of such a different flavor from before. Matilde looked at me, her eyes no longer frightened, only bemused. We were next to a window. The sun beat down on it, illuminating her face without shadow. She seemed drained, her face drooping, her breasts sagging, as if Orimbelli had worn her out in a few months.

Facing me but behind Matilde, a woman and a girl wearing black from head to toe sat at a table like ours. They'd returned from the funeral of their husband and father, respectively. The girl, not more than eighteen, stared at me as if into space, searching for her father's image. She had black hair, a pale and delicate face and a long neck, white and tender, which rose like the stem of a flower from a firm, decidedly statuesque bust. She was the very image of an orphan, as rendered by Cremona or Ranzoni.

I couldn't help but look at her. I moved from the slight roughness of her forehead to the dark down of her upper lip, and met her kind, grave regard, which she settled on me in order to avoid more painful sights. She was searching for that joie de vivre, which no young person can be robbed of for more than a day.

Matilde spoke faintly, perhaps to draw me away, since she'd understood the object of my distraction without having to turn round. "When will you come to the villa?"

"In a few days. As soon as I'm back from Milan."

After that, I couldn't manage to get another conversation going for the rest of the meal. I'd hoped to find a way to say good-bye to her, but nothing came to me as she was getting into the car other than the banal "See you soon."

I let two weeks go by before I returned to Oggebbio, where the *Tinca* was waiting for me in the dock at Villa Cleofe. I took a shuttle boat as far as Cannero, then walked along the main road so Cavallini wouldn't see me; he never missed the arrival of the boats or coaches. I walked through that beautiful summer morning, along the walls of the villas, in and out of the shadows of their grounds, looking at the lake dazzling in every cove below and at the opposite shore, which stood out black against the sun. The sun beat down on those paths and the perfume of the ferns and herbs that grew along them rose up to me; they seemed to burst from a mountainside swollen with greenery, which ended abruptly at the lake. Along those shadowy stretches, in the shelter of cedars, camphor and magnolia, I heard the sound of my steps on asphalt in front of the gates and small doors that punctuated the walls enclosing the villas, now mildewed and shut forever. My mind was blank, and I felt like a wayfarer habituated to long walks, always confident of finding a meal and a bed just waiting for someone without a home—someone wandering the world in good spirits, sure of finding it navigable, at times truly welcoming.

I got to the villa around eleven and found the gate open. Domenico was busy in the grounds, Martina surely in the kitchen and Lenin perhaps behind the gatehouse, occupied with some business of her own.

Matilde was on the terrace facing the lake, and I reached

her after crossing the whole of the ground floor without being seen by anyone.

She sat in the shade of the wisteria, in a large wicker armchair shaped like a hip bath close to the iron railings of the balustrade. She looked completely relaxed, like a convalescent on the terrace of a clinic: her head rested on a red cushion tied to the armchair and her forearms were stretched out on the armrests. Her hands hung loosely in the emptiness, seemingly pointing toward the pavement.

I circled the armchair and went to lean against the balustrade.

Her gaze, which had been surveying the great emptiness of the lake, refocused and settled on me.

"Good morning," I said. "Forgive me for not announcing myself, but I didn't see anyone between here and the gate."

She seemed not to be listening to my words. Without moving, but still looking at me as if she were dreaming, she murmured, "Take a chair and sit down here beside me."

I took a wicker chair similar to hers from under a cover and sat down next to her.

"So you're here," she said. And after a pause, "You'll have heard that Berlusconi left for Addis Ababa . . . "

"I haven't heard anything."

"Yes. He left—this time forever—after giving me the villa and everything in it. To make up for the damage caused by his negative impact on my future prospects."

"Then from now on you'll always live here?" I asked. "On your own?"

"Not on my own. With Domenico, Lenin and Martina . . ." She looked at me intently and added, "And with you, if you'd like."

I dropped my head and remained silent. My eyes on the pavement, I saw her rounded calves, crossed, and her rather wide feet in very narrow shoes. I knew she was waiting for my response, and that I ought to raise my head and give it to her one way or another.

I tried to imagine myself presiding over the Villa Cleofe, with the *Tinca* in the dock, Martina bringing me coffee in bed every morning, Domenico doffing his big straw hat at me when I crossed through the grounds and Lenin serving me at table, where I'd sit across from Matilde.

Meanwhile, I looked at her feet and asked myself how she could stand such tight shoes without pain.

But I couldn't sidestep the issue. Matilde, staring once more at the great emptiness of the lake, was waiting.

Sleeping . . . I'd usually sleep in the bishop's bedroom— to preserve my freedom and also because I knew Matilde loved being alone in her room; she'd always said so, even before marrying Orimbelli. The picture would be complete if, like a good husband, I showed up in the early morning or late at night, crossing the corridor in my pajamas and knocking discreetly at the door to her room.

I lifted my head and fixed my eyes on the lake. At that moment, the huge boat of Signor Kauffmann emerged like an apparition from the Cannero promontory. The *Lady* went by in silence, its four sails raised, its whiteness dazzling against the backdrop of the distant shore. The taut mainsail, mizzen, jib and flying jib, and the wall on the right completely hid everyone on board so that it seemed deserted. A few minutes later, the *Lady* rounded another promontory and disappeared.

It seemed to me that Signor Kauffmann's huge boat, appearing like a vision, had passed by to tell me that life is a mysterious journey, and that it was time for me to move on and call at other points, other ports.

I slowly got up and stood in front of Matilde. She raised her eyes to me.

"I'm going," I said. "Forgive me, but I must leave. I'm going down to the dock for the boat."

Ten minutes later I left the little dock of the Villa Cleofe in the *Tinca*. It was midday, and I decided to eat at Cavallini's Vittoria.

As I passed by the villa, I looked up at the terrace. Matilde had gone in. The only things visible between the iron bars of the baulstrade were the two wicker armchairs with their red headrests, the fringe on the cushions rustling in the wind.

I moored the boat in the harbor and climbed up to the road. Not a soul was about. The large balloons of trees spilling out from the gardens stood still under the sun. A hornet, stunned by the midday silence that had fallen over the lake and the houses, hummed through the pollen-laden air. I crossed over and stepped into the restaurant. I greeted Cavallini, who seemed to be waiting for me.

"It's been some time since I've had the pleasure of serving you!" he said.

"True. Since one evening in July last year. I was coming here to eat when I made the acquaintance of Signor Orimbelli at the port. The rest you know better than I do."

He seated me and remained thoughtful, the palms of his hands resting on my table. After a few moments, he brought his curly head close to mine and asked, "But now . . . are you coming back or are you on your way?"

"I'm leaving," I replied. "And it will be difficult for me to come back. I'm selling the boat. Getting off the lake."

"I'm sorry to hear that," he said quietly, "but I understand."

Then, looking around like a hawker flogging his goods, he began in a loud voice, "Today we have macaroni pie, a timbale of rice *alla finanziera*, cutlet *alla milanese*, ribs and fresh fish . . . "

When I left an hour later, Cavallini came to say good-bye at the harbor wall.

I moved swiftly toward the center of the lake, turning my back to the shore until, the inverna rising, I steered the prow toward the top of the lake and headed for my home port.

As soon as the *Tinca* began to pick up speed, I looked back toward the coast. I noted one villa after another, separated by their gardens: the Poss, the Ceriana, the Miralba, the Thea and then the Villa Cleofe, her spectral face veiled by the heat. My gaze moved on to the pasha's villa and the more modest one belonging to Massimo d'Azeglio. The wind shifted ninety degrees, and between Cannero and the mouth of Tresa, I sailed into home waters for the last time.

PIERO CHIARA (1913–1986) was a leading Italian author of the 20th century who won over a dozen literary prizes and whose work is marked by psychological depth, melancholy humor and a grasp of the essence of everyday life. *The Bishop's Bedroom* is the most celebrated of his many acclaimed novels.

JILL FOULSTON is the translator of novels by Erri de Luca, Augusto de Angelis and Piero Chiara. She lives in London.

THE 6:41 TO PARIS
BY JEAN-PHILIPPE BLONDEL

Cécile, a stylish 47-year-old, has spent the weekend visiting her parents outside Paris. By Monday morning, she's exhausted. These trips back home are stressful and she settles into a train compartment with an empty seat beside her. But it's soon occupied by a man she recognizes as Philippe Leduc, with whom she had a passionate affair that ended in her brutal humiliation 30 years ago. In the fraught hour and a half that ensues, Cécile and Philippe hurtle towards the French capital in a psychological thriller about the pain and promise of past romance.

OBLIVION
BY SERGEI LEBEDEV

In one of the first 21st century Russian novels to probe the legacy of the Soviet prison camp system, a young man travels to the vast wastelands of the Far North to uncover the truth about a shadowy neighbor who saved his life, and whom he knows only as Grandfather II. Emerging from today's Russia, where the ills of the past are being forcefully erased from public memory, this masterful novel represents an epic literary attempt to rescue history from the brink of oblivion.

THE YEAR OF THE COMET
BY SERGEI LEBEDEV

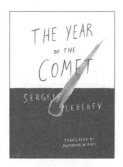

A story of a Russian boyhood and coming of age as the Soviet Union is on the brink of collapse. Lebedev depicts a vast empire coming apart at the seams, transforming a very public moment into something tender and personal, and writes with stunning beauty and shattering insight about childhood and the growing consciousness of a boy in the world.

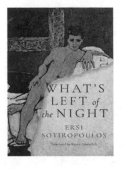

WHAT'S LEFT OF THE NIGHT
BY ERSI SOTIROPOULOS

Constantine Cavafy arrives in Paris in 1897 on a trip that will deeply shape his future and push him toward his poetic inclination. With this lyrical novel, tinged with an hallucinatory eroticism that unfolds over three unforgettable days, celebrated Greek author Ersi Sotiropoulos depicts Cavafy in the midst of a journey of self-discovery across a continent on the brink of massive change. A stunning portrait of a budding author—before he became C.P. Cavafy, one of the 20th century's greatest poets—that illuminates the complex relationship of art, life, and the erotic desires that trigger creativity.

AND THE BRIDE CLOSED THE DOOR
BY RONIT MATALON

A young bride shuts herself up in a bedroom on her wedding day, refusing to get married. In this moving and humorous look at contemporary Israel and the chaotic ups and downs of love everywhere, her family gathers outside the locked door, not knowing what to do. Is this merely a case of cold feet? A feminist statement? This provocative and highly entertaining novel lingers long after its final page.

A VERY FRENCH CHRISTMAS

A continuation of the very popular Very Christmas Series, this collection brings together the best French Christmas stories of all time in an elegant and vibrant collection featuring classics by Guy de Maupassant and Alphonse Daudet, plus stories by the esteemed twentieth century author Irène Némirovsky and contemporary writers Dominique Fabre and Jean-Philippe Blondel. With a holiday spirit conveyed through sparkling Paris streets, opulent feasts, wandering orphans, flickering desire, and more than a little wine, this collection proves that the French have mastered Christmas.

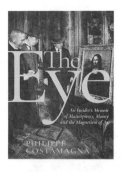

THE EYE
BY PHILIPPE COSTAMAGNA

It's a rare and secret profession, comprising a few dozen people around the world equipped with a mysterious mixture of knowledge and innate sensibility. Summoned to Swiss bank vaults, Fifth Avenue apartments, and Tokyo storerooms, they are entrusted by collectors, dealers, and museums to decide if a coveted picture is real or fake and to determine if it was painted by Leonardo da Vinci or Raphael. *The Eye* lifts the veil on the rarified world of connoisseurs devoted to the authentication and discovery of Old Master artworks.

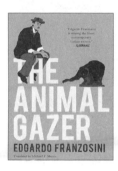

THE ANIMAL GAZER
BY EDGARDO FRANZOSINI

A hypnotic novel inspired by the strange and fascinating life of sculptor Rembrandt Bugatti, brother of the fabled automaker. Bugatti obsessively observes and sculpts the baboons, giraffes, and panthers in European zoos, finding empathy with their plight and identifying with their life in captivity. Rembrandt Bugatti's work, now being rediscovered, is displayed in major art museums around the world and routinely fetches large sums at auction. Edgardo Franzosini recreates the young artist's life with intense lyricism, passion, and sensitivity.

ALLMEN AND THE DRAGONFLIES
BY MARTIN SUTER

Johann Friedrich von Allmen has exhausted his family fortune by living in Old World grandeur despite present-day financial constraints. Forced to downscale, Allmen inhabits the garden house of his former Zurich estate, attended by his Guatemalan butler, Carlos. This is the first of a series of humorous, fast-paced detective novels devoted to a memorable gentleman thief. A thrilling art heist escapade infused with European high culture and luxury that doesn't shy away from the darker side of human nature.

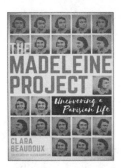

THE MADELEINE PROJECT
BY CLARA BEAUDOUX

A young woman moves into a Paris apartment and discovers a storage room filled with the belongings of the previous owner, a certain Madeleine who died in her late nineties, and whose treasured possessions nobody seems to want. In an audacious act of journalism driven by personal curiosity and humane tenderness, Clara Beaudoux embarks on *The Madeleine Project*, documenting what she finds on Twitter with text and photographs, introducing the world to an unsung 20th century figure.

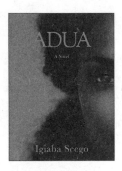

ADUA
BY IGIABA SCEGO

Adua, an immigrant from Somalia to Italy, has lived in Rome for nearly forty years. She came seeking freedom from a strict father and an oppressive regime, but her dreams of film stardom ended in shame. Now that the civil war in Somalia is over, her homeland calls her. She must decide whether to return and reclaim her inheritance, but also how to take charge of her own story and build a future.

IF VENICE DIES
BY SALVATORE SETTIS

Internationally renowned art historian Salvatore Settis ignites a new debate about the Pearl of the Adriatic and cultural patrimony at large. In this fiery blend of history and cultural analysis, Settis argues that "hit-and-run" visitors are turning Venice and other landmark urban settings into shopping malls and theme parks. This is a passionate plea to secure the soul of Venice, written with consummate authority, wide-ranging erudition and élan.

THE MADONNA OF NOTRE DAME
BY ALEXIS RAGOUGNEAU

Fifty thousand people jam into Notre Dame Cathedral to celebrate the Feast of the Assumption. The next morning, a beautiful young woman clothed in white kneels at prayer in a cathedral side chapel. But when someone accidentally bumps against her, her body collapses. She has been murdered. This thrilling novel illuminates shadowy corners of the world's most famous cathedral, shedding light on good and evil with suspense, compassion and wry humor.

THE LAST WEYNFELDT
BY MARTIN SUTER

Adrian Weynfeldt is an art expert in an international auction house, a bachelor in his mid-fifties living in a grand Zurich apartment filled with costly paintings and antiques. Always correct and well-mannered, he's given up on love until one night— entirely out of character for him—Weynfeldt decides to take home a ravishing but unaccountable young woman and gets embroiled in an art forgery scheme that threatens his buttoned up existence. This refined page-turner moves behind elegant bourgeois facades into darker recesses of the heart.

MOVING THE PALACE
BY CHARIF MAJDALANI

A young Lebanese adventurer explores the wilds of Africa, encountering an eccentric English colonel in Sudan and enlisting in his service. In this lush chronicle of far-flung adventure, the military recruit crosses paths with a compatriot who has dismantled a sumptuous palace and is transporting it across the continent on a camel caravan. This is a captivating modern-day Odyssey in the tradition of Bruce Chatwin and Paul Theroux.

EXPOSED
BY JEAN-PHILIPPE BLONDEL

A dangerous intimacy emerges between a French teacher and a former student who has achieved art world celebrity. The painting of a portrait upturns both their lives. Jean-Philippe Blondel, author of the bestselling novel *The 6:41 to Paris,* evokes an intimacy of dangerous intensity in a stunning tale about aging, regret and moving ahead into the future.

SLEEPLESS NIGHT
BY MARGRIET DE MOOR

A woman gets up in the middle of a wintry night and starts baking a Bundt cake while her lover sleeps upstairs. When it's time for her to take the cake out of the oven, we have read a tale of romance and death. The narrator of this novel was widowed years ago and is trying to find new passion. But the memory of her deceased husband and a shameful incident still holds her in its grasp. Why did he do it?

GUYS LIKE ME
BY DOMINIQUE FABRE

Dominique Fabre, born in Paris and a life-long resident of the city, exposes the shadowy, anonymous lives of many who inhabit the French capital. In this quiet, subdued tale, a middle-aged office worker, divorced and alienated from his only son, meets up with two childhood friends who are similarly adrift. He's looking for a second act to his mournful life, seeking the harbor of love and a true connection with his son. Set in palpably real Paris streets that feel miles away from the City of Light, a stirring novel of regret and absence, yet not without a glimmer of hope.

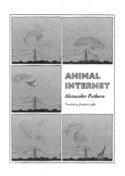

ANIMAL INTERNET
BY ALEXANDER PSCHERA

Some 50,000 creatures around the globe—including whales, leopards, flamingoes, bats and snails—are being equipped with digital tracking devices. The data gathered and studied by major scientific institutes about their behavior will warn us about tsunamis, earthquakes and volcanic eruptions, but also radically transform our relationship to the natural world. Contrary to pessimistic fears, author Alexander Pschera sees the Internet as creating a historic opportunity for a new dialogue between man and nature.

KILLING AUNTIE
BY ANDRZEJ BURSA

A young university student named Jurek, with no particular ambitions or talents, finds himself with nothing to do. After his doting aunt asks the young man to perform a small chore, he decides to kill her for no good reason other than, perhaps, boredom. This short comedic masterpiece combines elements of Dostoevsky, Sartre, Kafka, and Heller, coming together to produce an unforgettable tale of murder and—just maybe—redemption.

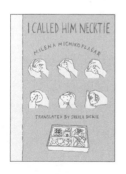

I CALLED HIM NECKTIE
BY MILENA MICHIKO FLAŠAR

Twenty-year-old Taguchi Hiro has spent the last two years of his life living as a hikikomori—a shut-in who never leaves his room and has no human interaction—in his parents' home in Tokyo. As Hiro tentatively decides to reenter the world, he spends his days observing life from a park bench. Gradually he makes friends with Ohara Tetsu, a salaryman who has lost his job. The two discover in their sadness a common bond. This beautiful novel is moving, unforgettable, and full of surprises.

 New Vessel Press

To purchase these titles and for more information
please visit newvesselpress.com.